Change of Breed

The Beginning

Other Works by Ashley Nicole

Sacrificial Lamb – The Other Angels Book One

Side Effects – A Sacrificial Lamb Novelette

Change of Breed

The Beginning

Ashley Nicole

Dark &
Twisted
Press

Published by
Dark and Twisted Press
P. O. Box 1064
Moorefield, WV 26836

ISBN 978-1-7347191-1-6
Library of Congress Control Number 2020920902

This is a work of fiction. Names, characters, businesses, places, events, locales, and incidents are either the products of the author's imagination or used in a fictitious manner. Any resemblance to actual persons, living or dead, or actual events is purely coincidental.

First Edition

Visit www.ashleynicolewrites.com to learn more.

This book is dedicated to my coworkers. Thank you for putting up with my endless zombie questions and enticing my imagination. Hopefully, this book is purely fictitious, and we will never have zombies crashing through our front doors, but if we do, just know, you've helped me prepare for it.

Chapter One

Sydney

The familiar, steady beeping of the surgical monitor lulls Sydney in and out of daydreaming. Dr. Will stands in front of her, on the other side of the surgical table, sowing up the spay incision of the unconscious Jack Russell lying on its back. The small room has light blue walls and a pale green floor. Bright spotlights hang from the ceiling and illuminate the belly of the dog. The surgical table, monitor, anesthesia cart, laser, and IV pump take up most of the space, making the room comfortable for only the tech and doctor.

"Any plans this weekend?" Will asks as he dabs a piece of gauze over the now closed incision. The older male doctor is in his late forties and confident in his abilities as a surgeon. His receding black hair and genuine interest in his techs' lives makes him feel father-like to Sydney. More of a father than her own anyway.

"Spencer and I are thinking of going hiking. The weather is supposed to be decent." Sydney unhooks the dog from the machines and carries it out into the treatment area. The same floor and wall colors cover the large rectangle room. Metal kennels line several of the walls and contain different patients. Four treatment tables take up most of the center of the room, their chrome tops dotted with rubbing alcohol bottles, disinfectant sprays, and baskets of blood tubes. "What about you?" she asks, laying the dog in her kennel. She begins clipping its nails.

Will makes some notes on the patient's anesthesia chart. "Well, if I ever remember to take home that horse trailer sitting outside, Erin and I are supposed to take some cows to an auction."

"That would be fun for your kiddos." The dog stirs, so Sydney averts her attention back to the disoriented patient and strokes its fur.

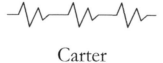

Carter

Carter stands in the pharmacy hallway connected to the treatment area, counting small white pills of Amoxicillin to fill a prescription.

Josie, the petite Calico office cat, hops onto the counter and meows for attention. Carter gives into the temptation and strokes her silky fur. Josie nudges his hand for more as Chris, the male receptionist, enters the pharmacy from the second of three doors leading to the lobby and lays a chart next to the computer.

"Mrs. Spruce says she has some questions about her tick medicine." Chris smiles with a knowing look in his dark brown eyes. His trimmed light brown hair and beard compliment his dapper dress style of a maroon polo and black dress pants.

Carter glances over the details on the chart such as name, age, and breed. "What kind of questions?" he asks.

"Oh, she's like all these other clients, worried about this new mosquito she seen on Facebook." Chris shakes his head and slides back through the door leading out front.

Carter blows out a sigh and opens the file for Bella, *how original*, and looks for any upcoming vaccines. He makes some quick notes on the chart then heads out through the first door leading to the lobby. He passes exam rooms one and two before his gaze lands on a young, hyper Chocolate Lab bouncing from the floor to the bench repeatedly, pulling on her owner's arm with the leash. The owner, a middle-aged woman, scrolls her thumb across her phone screen with glasses perched at the end of her nose. Her styled blonde hair barely moves with the jostling provided by her dog.

"I'm ready for Bella," Carter says with a smile. The woman looks up, giving him a once over, then places her phone and glasses in her purse before following. Carter leads her to room one, which is his favorite because of the large painted mural on the wall with lots of kittens romping together tangled in yarn. The small square exam room holds a scale, two chairs, and a counter with a sink and a computer. As Carter shuts the door, the woman already has her phone back out. "Hello, I'm Carter and I'm a tech. I need to get a weight and temp on Miss Bella." Carter leads the dog onto the lowered scale and watches as the numbers fluctuate, trying to gage an accurate weight on the wild pup.

"That tick medicine, does it protect from this?" The woman's voice is a higher pitch than Carter expected. She flashes her phone, the screen depicting a picture of a mosquito with a red head and three small red dots lining its back. Carter has seen a lot of these in the past week. There are lots of Facebook videos of people trying to identify them, having appeared from nowhere overnight.

"Your prevention is for fleas and ticks, not mosquitos, but I will double check with the doctor if there's anything you can do for protection against those." Carter pokes the lubed thermometer into the dog's rectum, stilling her chaotic behavior momentarily, then writes the normal temperature down on the chart. He launches into his regular questions about the diet and lifestyle of the dog, keeping notes on the chart, then politely exits the room promising a swift appearance of the doctor.

Carter enters the doctor's office just off the treatment area. Dr. Erin, Will's wife, sits at her desk typing away at her computer. The small room holds three desks for the doctors and numerous filing cabinets. A bookshelf tucked in the corner opposite the door overflows with medical journals and veterinary books. Erin glances out the single window until she hears the approaching footsteps. Her tight dark blonde ponytail swishes as she swivels her chair around to face Carter. "What do you have for me?" she asks as she stands to meet her tech at the doorway. Erin's expression is soft, and she wears minimal makeup.

Carter hands her the chart. "Mrs. Spruce has Bella, a six-month-old chocolate lab here for her wellness prior to spay. Weight and temp are normal, and all vaccines are up to date."

"Any concerns at home?" Erin asks as she looks over Carter's handwritten notes.

"The only concern she mentioned to me was about the new mosquito. She wants to know if her preventions will protect against it."

Erin shakes her head. "I think I've been asked that in every appointment for the past two weeks. There aren't many studies out on it yet. I'll tell her what I know. Lead the way."

Carter gives a half smile and leads Erin to room one. The woman is still scrolling through her phone when they walk in.

"Hello, Mrs. Spruce, I'm Dr. Erin. Hello Bella." Erin bends down to pet the lab's head. "I understand you want to have your girl checked out today for her spay? And Carter says you have some questions."

"Yes, this new mosquito." Mrs. Spruce shows Erin the picture on her phone. "It has been all over my Facebook feed and I don't want it harming Bella. Do I need another prevention?"

"There isn't a specific prevention available for mosquitos, but from what I've researched, there hasn't been any harm done to pets who come in contact with this species." Erin begins feeling along the dog, checking her lymph nodes in her neck before moving on to her abdomen and her hips while Carter restrains and distracts the dog's head. "I don't think the mosquito is a whole new species, but rather an invasive one. New studies should be coming out soon for us to know more."

"Should," Mrs. Spruce says in a mocking tone. "Do you have to Google all your answers?"

Carter's eyes widen but Erin continues as if the woman's comment wasn't out of line. "I'm part of several veterinary groups and we share information as it comes to us. This field is forever changing, so research is essential to staying on top of things."

Mrs. Spruce waves her hand and dismisses Erin's response. "Will you be performing the surgery on Bella?"

Erin pulls off her stethoscope from around her neck and listens to Bella's heart and lungs before answering. "That will be my husband, Dr. Will."

"Are you not capable of doing it yourself?"

A heat rises to Erin's cheeks, but she smiles. "I chose to pursue the wellness and diagnostic side of veterinary medicine rather than the surgical side. I assure you Bella is in good hands with Dr. Will." Erin looks in Bella's ears, eyes, and mouth.

"You don't do surgery and you're not sure about her preventions. I think I'd prefer seeing a more capable doctor next time." The woman drops her phone into her purse and pulls on Bella's leash. "Does she check out for surgery or should I get a second opinion?"

"She's all good to go." Erin mutters as she holds the door open.

Back in the treatment area, Carter sits at the tech desk near the doctor's office and makes a note in Mrs. Spruce's file to not put her with Erin again.

Erin walks by and places her hand on Carter's

shoulder. "Some people just have zero manners."

"Not doing surgeries doesn't make you an incapable doctor. I think you're great at what you do." He gives her a smile then continues recording his notes.

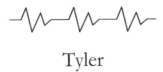

Tyler

Tyler wanders into the staff room sitting between the office and the long counter filled with blood and urine analysis machines in the treatment area. He picks up his cup to get a drink of now-cold coffee, thinking about lunch. Carter and Mason sit at the eight-chaired, scratched-up wooden table, scrolling through their phones and talking about the funny memes they find. The tomato soup for Mason's lunch boils on the stove, making Tyler's stomach rumble. Olivia emerges from the adjoining employee bathroom, flops onto the tan couch, and pulls out her own phone. Her pixie cut black hair falls in her face as she grabs a granola bar from her purse and begins munching. The screen of her phone reflects in her thick white framed glasses. One blue and one red hair scrunchie occupy her left wrist.

Tyler finishes his drink as Sara calls from a few feet away. "Tyler, can you help me get some blood?"

Tyler sets his cup down to go lend a hand. As he passes through the treatment area, a few sharp barks come from the hall housing the four runs for larger and noisier patients, with the laundry room tucked away at its end. Answering yaps come from the metal kennels filling any empty wall space. He weaves through the four treatment tables in the middle of the room. The pharmacy hall, with three doors spaced along a wall leading to the lobby, is opposite the run hallway and the glass back door leading outside.

Sara waits at one end of a treatment table. "Thanks, Dr. Heather wants to run some lab work on Chance." Her voice is honey sweet as she pulls the needed blood tubes from a basket on the table. "Do you mind grabbing him from the runs?"

Tyler nods and enters the narrow run hallway. On his right side are four tall kennels with glass fronts. Only two are occupied right now. Chance's barks from the farthest kennel bounce off the walls and make Tyler's ears ring in the confined space. He whistles to get the dog's attention to maybe quiet him as he makes his way past the other kennels. In the kennel before Chance's is another dog the doctors have been boarding for observation this week. Finn, a lovable and excited golden retriever has been showing strange behaviors according to the owner. Up until now, no one at the office has seen anything out of the ordinary.

Finn stands, facing Tyler. His body is hunkered down, and he bares his teeth. A low continuous growl rumbles from his throat. His eyes stare into Tyler's— not like he's just any threat, but with a ferocity implying immediate danger. Challenging him. The focused glare makes Tyler feel uncomfortable, and he breaks eye contact and shakes his head, making a mental note to ask Dr. Will about it later.

In the next kennel, Chance is the exact opposite. The white pit bull prances with excitement. His long tongue hangs out the side of his mouth, and his nubby tail wiggles with the rest of his butt. Tyler opens the door and tightens a slip lead around the dog's neck. He follows Tyler without hesitation past Finn and back to Sara.

Back in the treatment area, Tyler crouches down and makes Chance sit. He then restrains the head in a pointed-up position for Sara to draw blood from the jugular vein in the neck. As she pokes with her syringe, he notices a piece of her wavy brown hair falling in her face and thinks of what it would be like to tuck it behind her ear, to touch her face softly with his hand, to kiss her lips again. The longing makes his chest ache. He shakes the thought away. They're just friends. That's what she wants. Who was he to push?

Sara pulls out her needle and disperses the blood in the tubes. Tyler writes the dog's name on the tubes as Sara takes Chance to Heather. He walks by pharmacy as Melissa, one of the three receptionists, shoves the door open. "We have a walk-in ER. A dog was hit by a car. Its back legs are bleeding bad, and it's not breathing very good." She disappears back up front.

Tyler shoves away thoughts of lunch and goes up front to get the dog. It's a young black pit bull wrapped in a blue, blood-stained blanket in a man's arms. The male owner paces by the door, fear and panic written on his face. Tyler approaches them. "Hello sir, I'm Tyler. I understand your dog was hit by a car?"

The tall balding man chokes back a sob. "I didn't see him when I was backing out of the driveway. Usually he moves out of the way, but I was in a hurry and didn't make sure. He's my daughter's dog. He's a good boy. His name's Jake. Please fix him up, will ya?"

The man physically starts to shake as Tyler lifts the puppy out of his arms. The dog let's out a yelp of pain as Tyler repositions him. "We'll do our best. I'm going to take him straight to the doctors. Chris here will take you to an exam room." Tyler gestures to the nearby male receptionist who motions for the man to follow.

Tyler pushes one of the doors open to the treatment area and sets the dog gently down on a treatment table. "I need a doctor, I have an emergency, hit by car."

Erin pops out of the office having finished with her last appointment, unwrapping the stethoscope from around her neck. She pulls the blanket from the dog and listens to its chest. Now that Tyler can see the back legs, his heart sinks. One leg lays back at a wrong angle while several small bones stick out from around the paw. A pool of blood bleeds through the blanket. The sight itself doesn't unsettle him—he's seen worse—but the possible prognosis makes him ache for the dog and the owner. Erin checks a few more things then disappears back in the office. She returns with a syringe. Tyler holds off the vein on the front leg while Erin injects the sedation. Once Jake is sleepy, Erin scoops him up and crosses the treatment area. "Let's go shoot some x-rays. I want to make sure there's no internal bleeding, then I'll talk to the owner about the leg."

Tyler follows her to the x-ray room which is nestled between the surgery suite and CT room and puts on his protective weighted gown and dosimeter badge. As they stretch the dog out on its side, he asks, "Is the leg going to have to be amputated?"

"Most likely. I need to see if the damage is all in

the lower half or if it goes up into the hip as well," Erin says as she repositions the dog to take another picture.

"You'll just be a little furry tripod then, won't you boy?" Tyler chuckles.

After Erin gets all she needs, she studies the images on the computer as Tyler rubs the dog's head and waits. Erin turns back to him. "Okay, the knee and paw are shattered, but the hip and spine look intact and I don't see any internal bleeding. I'm going to go talk to the owner, do you know where he is?"

"I think Chris put him in room four." Tyler lifts the dog from the table to put him in a kennel where he can be more comfortable. While Erin hustles to the exam room to relay her findings, Tyler thinks of the surgery to come and strokes Jake's fur. "It's going to be okay."

Chapter Two

Sydney

The full moon sits high in the night sky. Its brightness illuminates the gravel path thirteen-year-old Sydney tiptoes on. The air is thick and smells of summer rain. Even though she is only dressed in shorts and a t-shirt, sweat beads at the back of her neck.

The path leads her to her dad's kennel house. Inside, eight dogs doze in their cages, their fur patchy and bloodied. King is the first dog Sydney reaches. He's a bulky pit bull with short black fur. His head lifts as she approaches, and he lets out a warning growl. Sydney's heart pounds in her chest, but she creeps closer to the cage. She reveals a keyring and unlocks the padlock. As she unlatches the metal bar holding the cage door shut, she looks back at King. "It's okay, boy. I'm going to help you."

A wave of confidence runs over her. *The dogs have*

to sense I'm trying to help. Carefully she lowers herself to her knees and reaches out a tentative hand. King watches her with steely grey eyes. It feels like an eternity passes before Sydney's hand reaches King's coarse fur. She lets out the breath she was holding as he allows her to stroke him.

Suddenly, a bright light shines down on their private moment. King's fur bristles and he sinks back into the cage.

"What the hell do you think you're doing?" The angry male voice causes the fear to surge back. She turns her head to see her dad and his friends enter the kennel house. When Sydney doesn't answer or move, her dad grabs her arm. She lets out a squeal at the pain beneath his strong hand. King barks, and her dad kicks the cage. The dog leaps forward, teeth bared, searching for blood. His mouth latches onto Sydney's arm. Pain radiates through her limb. Her dad kicks King in the head, forcing him to release her.

Hot tears stream down her face as another strong arm jerks her back. She stumbles, off-balance, but she can't take her eyes off the large black dog. Someone tries to look at her bloodied arm, but she fights against them as her dad raises his pistol. The sharp pop continues to ring in her ears even as she wakes up, ten years later, drenched in sweat in her own bed. She reaches beside her to feel the warm presence of Spencer's sleeping body.

His phone begins to buzz for the 7:00 alarm. He grumbles and flops over to shut it off then reaches for Sydney. His arm wraps around her waist. "Good morning beautiful." His voice is heavy with sleep.

"Good morning," she mumbles, still fretting over

the images left in her head.

He must hear the fear in her voice because he pulls at her side for her to roll over and face him. "What's wrong?"

"I had a dream about when I lived with dad."

"The one with the dog?" His voice is as gentle as his fingertips rubbing the faint scars on her left forearm.

She nods and lets the tears come again. Spencer pulls her in tight, and they stay that way until his second alarm for 7:30 breaks the silence. When he turns it off this time he gets out of bed and switches on the tall lamp in the corner. They both get dressed and ready for work before moseying downstairs. He pours Sydney a cup of coffee in a travel mug as she pulls on a jacket and grabs her purse.

Spencer leans in to kiss her then makes her look at him. Her eyes trace the black stubble along his jawline until they reach his soft blue eyes full of love. "You're okay, Sydney. Your dad isn't here, and you heal animals now. All that's gone."

Sydney nods because she knows he's right. The nightmares still come, but that's all they are. Echoes of memories best forgotten. They say their goodbyes and leave for work.

Lynn

"I am so tired of you spending all your time at that place!" Daniel yells after Lynn as she attempts to get out the door faster.

"It's my job! I'll be fired if I don't go," she pleads. Her heart thunders as his heavy footsteps approach.

"You work when you're scheduled. I don't want you going in early or coming home late anymore. Got it?"

Lynn's shaky hands fumble with her keyring as she tries to single out the car key. Daniel grabs her shoulder and spins her around to face him. His ox-like form towers over her and his dark eyes drill into hers.

She squirms. "Yeah."

"Lucas!" Daniel shouts without letting go of Lynn.

A small five-year-old boy tentatively peaks around the corner from the living room. "Yes?"

"Leave him out of this." Tears sting Lynn's eyes.

"Shut up!" Daniel roars then looks back to Lucas. "What have I said about saying 'yeah' instead of 'yes'?"

"That it's disrespectful," the child mumbles.

"Right." Daniel slaps his hand across Lynn's face. "So, learn some respect and be home at five."

He shoves her toward the front door, and she holds her hand over her cheek.

Driving down the road, Lynn resists the urge to speed. She wasn't expected at work for another hour, but she had to lie to Daniel just to get out of the house. She turns the radio up for a distraction. "Break-ins are at an all-time high this week." She flips the channel. "Welcome to pet corner where we help you find your missing pet and boy, do we have a very long list for you today!" She flips the channel again. "Patients are complaining of hearing voices. Is this a new type of schizophrenia?" Finally, she flips the station and pop music fills the car. She turns it up and clears her thoughts.

A few short minutes later, she pulls into the gravel parking lot of Second Chance Animal Hospital. Looking at the brown and tan building, she smiles to herself. She flips down her sun visor and opens the mirror to assess her appearance. Her cheek is still a little red, so she pulls her concealer from her purse and reapplies a light dusting of the powder. She touches up the rest of her makeup and fluffs her blonde waves before exiting her car. She knows she wears too much makeup for her job, but it makes her feel pretty since her husband doesn't.

Once inside, the lobby opens to the main front counter accommodating two receptionists—Chris, a middle-aged man who is always smiling, and Melissa, a laid-back woman who enjoys superhero movies and fantasy novels. On Lynn's right, she catches a glimpse of Carla's thick curly hair through the grooming room's viewing window bobbing to music as she shaves a fluffy black Pomeranian. Lynn heads for the leftmost door leading to the treatment area. Susan, the elderly third receptionist, waves a good morning from the connected retail area as she tidies up some of the brightly colored leashes and plushy toys.

Lynn pushes open the door and observes the actions around her. Olivia is holding a small tan Chihuahua while Tiffany skillfully goes through trimming its nails. Tyler and Carter are over at the surgical prep table shaving a dog for surgery for Will. Lynn takes her purse and lunch to the staff room as Mason comes out of the connected employee bathroom. His tall muscular body has always been more attractive to her than her husband's bulky one. She also loves the rich orange color of his short hair and beard. His large, dark green eyes invite her into their murky depths. "Hey Lynn, how are you today?"

Lynn stiffens at the loaded question but smiles. "I'm good, how are you?"

"I'm alright, it's been a quiet morning here." Mason leans over to rap his knuckles on the wooden cabinet to un-jinx himself from saying the Q word in the clinic.

Lynn goes back out to the treatment area and over to the kennel where a now three-legged Jake sits with his tongue hanging out in a doggy smile. She slips a few fingers through the bars which are met by his wet nose. "Hey buddy, how are you feeling today?" His head tilts sideways as she speaks, sending one of his floppy ears over to lay on top his head. His amputation surgery a few days ago went well, and today is the day he gets to return to his little girl.

Melissa brings back a chart for an appointment and Lynn falls into the normal rhythm of work. The two dogs in the runs start a barking competition with each other so she escapes to the quiet of the lobby to greet her first patient of the day.

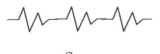

Sara

Fog sits heavy on the surrounding landscape as Sara navigates her dark grey Toyota Prius down the quiet back road just outside town. Her limited vision gives her the illusion of being trapped in a bubble. The wail of the sirens reaches her ears before she sees the flashing red lights of an ambulance sneaking up behind her, seemingly out of nowhere in the dense fog. She quickly pulls her car off to the side of the road to let the emergency vehicle speed pass and watches it vanish in the distance. *Who's headed to the hospital?*

She begins driving again, and a soft giggle from the back seat makes her look in her rearview mirror. Mila squeezes the head of her stuffed chicken and kicks her feet in her car seat. Sara smiles and returns her eyes to the road. Two black labs stand on the yellow line, and she slams on the breaks in order to not hit them. Her six-month-old daughter lets out a string of sobs, the sudden jolt having scared her.

Sara looks away from the dogs to reach her hand in the backseat to comfort Mila. She rubs her daughter's leg and tries to maneuver the pacifier into her mouth. Mila gladly accepts the offering and sucks on the binky.

Satisfied the crisis is averted, Sara looks back at the dogs. Her heart jumps in her chest and a gasp escapes her lips as she notices they're closer. One still stands in the road only inches from the hood of her car. The other has shifted to the driver's side and glares at her through the window. The unsettling feeling makes her hand raise slowly to the horn. She beeps it a few times, but the dogs don't flinch. She taps her foot on the gas, revving her engine, but there's still no reaction.

She glances down at her phone to find someone to call. Anyone. Her fear rises even though she doesn't fully understand why. When she looks back up, the dogs are gone. Sighing in relief, she continues to the babysitter's house.

When she drops Mila off, she takes a few extra minutes to savor the cuddles of her daughter. No matter the shame around her conception, this beautiful, brown-eyed girl will never be a mistake to her. With one last kiss, she reluctantly leaves to go to work.

Sara bustles through the front door of the animal hospital into the lobby. "I'm so late," she mutters to herself as she hurries to the back.

"Is everything okay?" Tiffany asks, sweeping her long black hair up into a ponytail.

Sara hastily throws her purse onto the couch in the staff room then quickly recaps the eventful drive to her best friend. "It was weird."

Tiffany wraps her olive toned arms around Sara and pulls her in for a hug. Sara gladly accepts the embrace, squeezing the shorter girl just as hard. "Sounds like it. I'm glad you're okay though. You haven't missed much this morning."

Tyler walks into the staff room as Sara and Tiffany release each other and places his tanned hand lightly on Sara's shoulder. "I'm glad to see you're okay too. How's Mila?"

Sara is very conscious of the light presence of Tyler's fingers. She thinks of shrugging them off but doesn't. His familiarity is still comforting. "She's good. I think the break check startled her, but she was safely strapped into her seat so no worries."

"You know, I could take her to the babysitter's some mornings so you can have some time to yourself if you ever need it." His almond-shaped brown eyes remind her of Mila's as they shine with hopefulness.

"Thanks." Sara gives a soft smile but hustles through the treatment area toward the surgery prep table to help Carter carry a large unconscious Golden Retriever into surgery.

They lay the ninety-pound dog onto the table and begin restraining his legs. "Thanks," Carter says. "Tyler was supposed to help but disappeared when he saw you come in." He enters the patient's information into the surgical monitor.

"No problem. I actually wanted to talk to you today. It was luck that I saw you struggling just now." Sara's nose crinkles with a teasing smile.

"What did you need to talk about?" Carter asks casually.

With his back to her, Sara takes a moment to admire his lean body, his shaggy blonde hair, the way his long fingers lightly dance over the buttons of the monitor. Then he's looking at her and she falls into the deepness of his hazel eyes. She follows the path of freckles over the tanned skin of his strong jaw.

His smooth voice brings her back. "Sara?"

She blinks a few times then feels heat rise to her cheeks. "Sorry, I must have gone off into space. Anyway, I was wondering if you were going to be busy tomorrow evening. I had plans with my sister but then she cancelled, and I already booked the time with my babysitter, so I thought…" Sara's voice trails off as she searches for the right words to continue.

Carter stiffens. "Are you asking me on a date?"

"Sorta, yeah, if you're free." Sara's soft tone is hopeful.

Carter shifts his weight from one foot to the other. "Oh, uh, well…"

"Carter and I are actually volunteering at a shelter tomorrow."

Sara turns around to see Sydney standing outside the doorway of the surgery room. She twists a ring on her finger nervously and her pale blue eyes dart between Carter and Sara. Sara takes in Sydney's fair skin and straight blonde hair. *She has a boyfriend and now she wants Carter too?*

Sara shifts her face behind a curtain of her brown hair to hide her disappointment. "Oh, yeah, sure, no big deal. Let me go tell Will you're ready for him." She turns for the door to exit the embarrassing situation she set up for herself.

Tiffany

The early afternoon brings much of the same as the quiet morning. The unusually large number of cancelations and no shows leaves a gap in the schedule. Surgeries are finished for the day, and soft chit chat carries out from the office as the three doctors discuss new studies and technologies. The techs revel in the downtime and crowd around Tyler who sits at the tech desk in the treatment area watching a funny YouTube video on the computer.

Tiffany hangs to the back of the group, leaning against one of the treatment tables, scrolling through Facebook. Phones are supposed to stay in the staff room, but the bosses aren't paying any mind. She passes several pictures in her news feed of dogs and people dressed up in tattered clothes. *September is a bit too early for posting Halloween costumes, isn't it?* Her phone buzzes with an incoming text. She sighs, knowing who it is. Brent's number shows at the top with a single text reading,

You got it yet?
2:35pm

Tiffany types back a quick reply hoping to hold him off.

Not yet, haven't been able
to get in the office
without being watched.
2:36pm

Her phone buzzes almost immediately.

You said you'd get it.
Are you holding out on
me?
2:36pm

No! If I'm caught, your
connection to your fix is
broken. I have to be
careful. Got it?
2:36pm

I better have it by the
end of the day.
2:37pm

Tiffany resists the urge to hurl her phone against the wall. Each time she goes into the doctor's office to look through the controlled drugs cabinet, a doctor walks in. Her job isn't worth this asshole's threats.

The UPS delivery man opens the back door and sets down several small brown cardboard boxes on the floor. He scans each label with his handheld machine and waves at Tiffany as he leaves. *Finally, something to do.*

Tiffany retrieves a box cutter and opens the first package. She scans over the packing slip and her eyes grow wide. Under the tightly packed bubble wrap is a bottle of Hydrocodone tablets. The opioid pain pills could be her answer. All she would have to do is get rid of the packing slip and the box and act like they were never received. No one is looking. She could walk out with the bottle without anyone noticing for days, and by then, the evidence would be gone.

Sydney

Sydney stands with her friends as they laugh at a video of a vet tech comedian ranting about clients putting their cats in everything but cat carriers when coming to the vet. She can't tell if she's imagining it or if Sara is giving her sidelong glares from where she stands. Sydney can't keep lying for Carter. He needs to come clean and tell Sara she's not his type before it gets anymore awkward.

A loud scream rips through the building, and silences Sydney's thoughts. Will pokes his head out of the doctor's office. "What the hell was that?"

Lynn reaches for the door leading out front, but more screams freeze her steps. Erin and Heather hover behind Will, who now blocks the office entry with his broad frame. The rest of the techs huddle around the tech desk and exchange worried glances. A chorus of barks circles the group with most of them coming from upfront, but the patients in their metal kennels don't hesitate to join in. The sound of a window shattering brings a new round of fear in Sydney's chest.

Gunshots inside the building pierce the air. Round after round, the deafening bangs ring out. Sydney clamps her hands over her ears and watches as the girls around her do the same. Sara grabs Tiffany's arm and buries her face into her shoulder. Mason shifts to where Lynn still stands and peeks out the window down the hall, his former military experience appearing to put him on alert. His eyes grow wide and he bolts away from the door, pulling Lynn along.

There's a quick shout of "Police!" then the door flings open and three police officers scan the room with pistols ready. Their uniforms are dirty. A mix of dirt and blood darkens the blue material. Will approaches them with his hands up as a sign of surrender. "What's going on here? What were all those screams?"

The closest police officer aims his gun at Will's chest. His jaw is set on his hard face. "Is anyone here sick? Has anyone been bitten?"

Will's eyes bounce over his employees' faces and then return to the officer's. "I don't think so, what's going on?"

The officer ignores his question again. "Everyone needs to stay here. Don't go outside and don't let anyone in. Officer Chase is going to stay with you until we can get you all out." He and one other officer turn for the door. Sydney exchanges an unsure glance with some of the techs around her.

Officer Chase stiffens for a moment but then

composes himself. "Yes, sir." He eyes the glass back door warily but stands his ground. The brown scruff on his face and his light blue eyes give him the appearance of being younger than the other two officers.

Mason speaks up before the men can leave. "Excuse me sir, but I'm a little confused as to what's going on. Why do we need an officer stationed here?"

"Officer Chase will explain everything. Right now, we need to head to the next building and see what we can accomplish." The officer gives a curt nod then exits with his partner.

With the other officers gone, the threat level lightens, and Erin nudges Will. He steps forward to stand directly in front of Officer Chase and looks him in the eyes, unblinking. In an authoritative voice, he demands, "What is happening in my hospital?"

Officer Chase doesn't answer immediately, and Sydney begins to wonder if he even will, but then he lets out a heavy sigh. "I might as well tell you, because I'm starting to think this situation is only going to get worse. First off though, I should let you know, everyone upfront is dead."

Sydney clamps a hand over her mouth. Overlapping questions burst from around her as her friends ask, "what do you mean?" and "everyone?" and "how can they be dead?" Sydney's pulse thumps in her ears like the heavy beat of a bass drum.

"What do you mean they're dead? Did you shoot them all?" Will's hands ball into fists at his sides, and stomps forward even more in the face of the officer until their chests are almost touching. The rest of the group quiets down to hear his explanation.

Keeping his voice calm, Officer Chase puts some space between him and Will by stepping toward the door he came through and peering out its window toward the lobby. "No, we killed the things that killed them. There are rabid dogs and crazed people out there who are sick, or on drugs, or something. Both are being caught breaking into buildings and people's homes and biting and *eating* them. It's sick."

"When did this start?"

"Hold up!" Officer Chase raises his gun. "Open the door slowly." He doesn't look at Will as he speaks.

"The cops are this crazed over a rabid dog?" Sara whispers under her breath.

"He said *dogs*. How many do you think there are?" Carter asks, voice just as hushed. No one answers.

Will turns the handle and eases the door open. The huddle around Sydney collectively leans, trying to see what is coming. Mrs. Croft from exam room three pokes her grey-haired head through the doorway, clutching her terror-stricken cat against her chest with her wrinkled hands. The white feline squirms, wide eyed, but it's a futile struggle in her owner's iron grip.

"Have you been bitten?" Officer Chase doesn't lower his gun.

"My Angel would never bite me." Mrs. Croft stares, offended and confused.

"What about by a dog or human? Did one of those things bite you?"

Mrs. Croft glances around the room, taking in all our worried expressions, before replying, "I've never owned a dog and I've never had a soul bite me, nor have I had a gun in my face. And that can cease right now."

Officer Chase lowers his gun and motions for Will to close the door once again. "I'm sorry, ma'am. It's hard to trust anyone right now when no one wants to admit they've been bitten."

"What in Heaven's name are you talking about? I heard screams and gunshots and my Angel dove under the chairs. I had a heck of a time getting her out. Now you're telling me you're the one going around shooting people? Are you robbing the place?" Mrs. Croft's hold on her cat tightens. *Can she even breathe?*

Sydney's head spins as she tries to wrap her mind around the situation. *Are we all going to be okay?*

"Ma'am, I'm a cop. I'm not robbing the place. I'm trying to protect everyone here from the things outside trying to kill you. Pointing fingers and worrying about your damn cat isn't going to help anyone. What we need is to stay calm and try to find a way to stay safe until backup arrives."

"Says the guy who keeps pointing a gun at us," Olivia mumbles, and Tyler elbows her.

"How long are we supposed to wait?" Will points a finger at the officer. "Your group said to stay here until they can get us out. Is that hours? Days? Longer?"

Sydney feels a hand lace its fingers through hers. She hadn't realized she was trembling until she looks, finding Carter and feeling him squeeze her hand. She takes a deep breath and gives him a squeeze back. *We're fine. We'll figure this out.*

Officer Chase's gaze grows dark as he levels a serious look at Will. "You don't know what it's been like out there this morning. What those things are capable of doing. I don't know how widespread all this is, but until it's safe, I am keeping you all here, however long that takes."

Chapter Three

Day one
Tyler

Tyler squeezes in between Tiffany and Carter as everyone crowds around Will, who now types away at the tech computer. Mrs. Croft passes her cat off to Olivia so she can cram in closer to the screen. Officer Chase paces the length of the room, talking in a hushed voice to his partners on his handheld radio. Lynn, Sara, and Erin dial numbers feverishly over and over on their cells, but it doesn't seem like they've gotten through to anyone.

"I think the cell towers are down." Lynn shoves her phone into her scrub pocket and reaches for the office phone. After a few seconds she slams it down on the receiver. "Landlines too."

"How am I supposed to know if Mila's okay?"

Tears slip down Sara's face as her obvious fear of the unknown surrounding her young daughter causes her body to shake. Her breathing comes out in short gasps.

Erin goes to Sara's side and puts her arms around her. "We're going to figure this out. Will's pulling up the news now. Maybe this will all be handled shortly. I'm sure your babysitter is keeping Mila perfectly safe."

Tyler thinks of going to Sara and wrapping his arms around her thin frame, but he knows he's not who she wants. Instead, he tries to lighten the mood. "Don't worry Sara, Mila's fine. The loud rumble of your Prius scared all the dogs away this morning."

Olivia snickers, but everyone else ignores the comment. *Lighten up, people.*

Will's video stream finally plays and consumes everyone's attention. A man in a brown suit sits at the news counter with a grim look. "Reports are coming in from Mercy, Grace, Handoff, Price, and other surrounding counties' sheriff departments. Officials are saying dogs and humans are being observed acting strange and aggressive. Police urge everyone to stay indoors and not to let anyone in until they can contain the situation. Right now, only confirmed sightings have been observed in dogs and humans, but to be safe, stay away from any suspicious wildlife. We don't know—"

All at once, the computer, lights, and lab equipment perpetually humming in the background shut off. Officer Chase pulls his gun up and calls to the other officers who confirm they're seeing the same. Light streams in from the high windows and the glass back door, causing shadows to fall across everyone's faces. A small yelp of fear escapes someone's lips. The group around Tyler huddles closer.

"You've got to be kidding me." Tiffany walks away from the group and stands with her back turned.

"Kidding about what?" Carter slumps against the wall.

"You guys don't see this is the fucking zombie apocalypse happening right now?" Tiffany whips around to face the group, her dark eyes serious.

"Yeah? And I'm a vampire." Tyler raises his hands into claws and hisses at Olivia as if he were going to bite her neck. She gives him a playful shove while still holding Angel.

"Don't be ridiculous…" Erin's voice trails off not convinced of her own dismissive comment.

Tiffany points to the door that leads to the lobby. "There's people outside biting and eating people. Aside from the plot twist with the dogs, I don't know what else to call it."

Tyler rolls his eyes. No one speaks. Erin looks to Will for answers. As they all muddle through their thoughts, Mrs. Croft snatches Angel from Olivia's arms. "This is foolish. Whatever those people are out there, they know we're in here. We have cars, so why don't we just leave?" She turns away, heading for the door.

Officer Chase points his gun at her. "I can't let you leave."

"And what are you going to do? Shoot me?" Mrs. Croft scoffs.

"If I have to, to keep everyone safe, I will." His facial expression doesn't waver. Tyler wonders how serious his threat is.

Mrs. Croft levels a glare at him. "Then what would make you any different than those things outside?"

He doesn't answer. No one says anything. Mrs. Croft seems to take the silence as acceptance and opens the door to the lobby. It clicks shut before anyone jolts back to reality. Officer Chase is the first to react, opening the door and pursuing the client down the hall past exam rooms three and four. Will follows on his heels with Erin close behind. The rest of the staff file behind in a disorganized bunch.

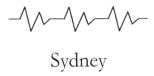

Sydney

In the lobby, red speckles decorate the white tiled floor, creating breadcrumb trails to the larger pools of blood. There are bodies, human and canine, laying everywhere, but Sydney forces herself not to look. The strong iron smell of blood stings her nose. There's something else too. A rotting aroma so intense, Sydney feels like she's stuck her head in the stomach of a surgery pet that's been sitting open for a week. She swallows the bile rising in her throat. An inhuman wail rises behind Sydney, and she turns to find Sara doubling over. Lynn and Olivia herd her back into the treatment area.

"Ma'am, you need to stay here. I can't protect you out there and leave this group unattended. It's not safe." Officer Chase reaches for the woman, but she twists away from him.

"I'll tell you what's not safe. Sitting here like prizes in a claw machine. I'm going to my car, and I'm leaving this sardine can." She turns on her heels and pushes the main doors open. Hairline cracks cover the glass door and the window to either side. Those left in the group that didn't retreat to the treatment area inch forward to watch her departure.

She takes her time attaching Angel's collar to one of those pet seatbelt leashes in the backseat of her tan SUV. Coming around the corner of the building, Sydney spies a figure accompanied by three dogs—a German Shepherd and two husky mixes still sporting their collars. The man walking with them walks with a limp, and his left arm is missing from elbow down, but no blood pours from the wound. *How is that possible?* His clothes are tattered from a struggle, with red claw marks peeking through the fabric. Every few steps, his head twitches.

"Look." Sydney points then watches Officer Chase's lips pinch together as the pained expression consumes his face. The color drains from her face as the realization sinks in. She reaches for the door handle, but Officer Chase snatches her hand away. She fights against him, but his strength makes her struggle useless. She watches in wide-eyed horror as the dogs draw closer to the oblivious client. A scream crawls its way up her throat. "Watch out!" Someone's hand clamps over her mouth. In the corner of her eye, Mason goes for the door. A breeze brushes across Sydney's face as he opens it.

"Don't go out there, they're about to swarm!" Officer Chase orders. "Shut the door."

"I can't just let that woman die." Mason looks to Mrs. Croft as if he's judging the distance from the building to the car.

"She'll get away if she ever gets in the damn car. But we won't if they decide to surround the building.

Now get back, or you're putting us all at risk." The officer's words have the desired effect, and Mason allows the door to ease closed, but his brow knits in regret.

Mrs. Croft must have heard something because her head whips around, and she lets out a shrill scream at the sight of her nearing company. She flings her driver's door open and climbs into the seat, slamming the door shut as the attackers reach her car. They let out a string of moans and snarls before scratching on the side of her car. The man reaches for the door, but a strong muscle tremor makes it look impossible for him to grip the handle. *Hopefully, she thought to lock it.* The German Shepherd jumps up on the hood and begins pawing at the glass. One of the Huskies begins to sniff under the vehicle.

As Mrs. Croft settles herself, she rummages through her purse to retrieve her car key and sticks it into the ignition. She tries turning the switch, but the motor doesn't turn on. The revving of the engine sputters again as she desperately twists on the key.

The noise attracts two more people and a small Chihuahua from near the staff's cars on the other side of the parking lot. They migrate toward the racket obscuring most of Mrs. Croft's car from view.

Relief floods through Sydney as the engine roars to life. Mrs. Croft floors it in reverse and pulls out of her parking spot, knocking away her attackers. The dog on the hood fumbles to the ground but instantly gets up and begins barking. Mrs. Croft shifts the car into drive and leaves, running over the foot of the one-armed man. The pain the impact should have elicited doesn't faze him and he hobbles after the car.

The dogs sniff and circle where the car was parked. The Shepherd gives one sharp bark and the rest look at him. A silent conversation seems to take place between them. The group inside the clinic stays motionless waiting for the animals to make a move. The Shepherd turns its head, and Sydney swears its looking right at her. Her heart rate quickens. Then, it turns away. The rest of the dogs follow to the employee cars. They each dive under the cars then emerge to move onto the next one.

"Son of a bitch," Officer Chase breathes.

"What's going on? What are they doing?" Mason looks at the door again like he wants to chase the dogs away himself.

"I don't know yet, but let's go back into the other room. We need walls between us."

Sydney lets her body go limp as the adrenaline pumping in her veins dies. No one says anything until they're back in the treatment area. She slumps into the tech desk chair. Everyone else either stands or sits on the floor as they wait for Officer Chase to talk. Sara's face is pale, and she stares at nothing.

The young police officer clears his throat. "We had been getting calls about these people and dogs breaking into houses all morning. We heard the stories from other cities, so we tried to prepare. When they saw us using dogs against them, they targeted our K9s. Then when they took an officer down, they would take their gun and run."

"Wait. It sounds like you're saying the dogs and people are planning together." Mason begins to pace.

Sydney's stomach churns. Her mind floods with the images left behind by this morning's dream. Fear.

Blood. Pain. Fur. Helplessness. Gunshots. The bile rises again but she swallows it back.

Officer Chase's expression grows dark. "I know that sounds crazy, but I don't know how else to explain it. When they see us do something, they learn it, and take it away. They did something to our cars outside, I don't know what, but they're not letting us leave as easily as that woman."

$$\sim\!\!\wedge\!\!\sim\!\!\wedge\!\!\sim$$

Tiffany

"Someone's got to say the obvious." Tiffany leans against the wall, arms folded across her chest.

"And what would that be?' Heather asks angrily.

"We're stuck. If we go outside, we'll be eaten. The vehicles don't work. The phones are down. We're on our own." She shoves her hands into the pockets of the jacket covering her scrub top, careful not to rattle the bottle of pills still stashed away. *Maybe Brent's dead, and I won't have to steal these after all.*

Sara raises an eyebrow. "How do we really know all the vehicles don't work? Maybe we can all just leave like Mrs. Croft."

Tiffany extends her arm gesturing toward the parking lot. "I want to get out of here too Sara, but you didn't see the dogs after Mrs. Croft left. They were communicating somehow. They want us to be trapped."

"Zombies don't think, they just eat." Olivia shakes her head and walks toward the staff room rubbing her temples.

"They're not zombies. This isn't some game or movie. These are rabid dogs and doped up people." Officer Chase perches on one of the treatment tables.

"I don't much care for what you think. I've seen a lot of people on every drug imaginable, and they didn't do shit like this. And rabid dogs don't ban together and make plans. You weren't going to lift a finger to help Mrs. Croft, so thank God her car did work, or she'd be dead because of you." Tiffany shoves her finger into the cop's face.

Officer Chase stands up, towering over Tiffany and looks her dead in the eye before replying in a low, steady voice. "Listen here. Out there right now are dozens of those things. Whatever they're on heightens their sense of smell and hearing. Whenever they smell blood, they swarm. When they hear noise, they swarm. If I went out there, I'd be dead, and you all wouldn't have a gun. You don't understand what they're capable of doing. Our department has been fighting our way through these things trying to get to every house, every business we can, so a little more respect for my decisions, however difficult and unfair they seem, would be appreciated." The man turns away, leaving Tiffany momentarily stunned.

"So, what do we do?" Heather's amber eyes bounce between Will and Erin, looking for answers.

"If it's survival we're facing, we should take stock of what supplies we have." Mason speaks up.

"That's a good idea." Will pulls a blank sheet of paper from the printer beside him and slides a pen out of his shirt pocket. "Since we run off a well pump, we don't have running water. See how many cases of bottled water we have, count canned and bagged foods—things we don't have to cook to eat—and look for anything we can use for defense. I think there's still some shovels in the CT room from winter. Maybe we will only be here for a couple hours, but taking inventory will give us something to do to pass the time."

Chapter Four

Day one
Lynn

Two full forty-eight packs of water and one missing a few bottles sit on the table in the staff room, along with all the cans of beans, corn, and carrots. Piles of crackers, granola bars, chips, and snack cakes make it look more like a party than a survival inventory. Will makes a note of all the things they have and instructs on how it should be divided to stretch it out the farthest. Lynn takes a sip of her first of two allotted bottles of water for the day.

Olivia comes into the staff room and eyes the sweets. "I don't understand why we can't just eat something if we're hungry. They act like we're going to be here for weeks." She crosses her arms and flops onto the couch.

"We could be. The police didn't say when they would be back, and we don't have a way to leave." Lynn pulls a Sharpie from her pocket and marks her initials on her water bottle. Although Olivia has been a godsend around the clinic the past few months she's been here, her high school age sometimes makes her act young and defiant.

"We can't really stay here that long."

"What else can we do?" she asks, not to Olivia but herself. *How long can we wait? How long can we survive if no one comes? At least I'm stuck here instead of at home.*

The sound of an engine near the back door makes the two techs look up. With the streets quiet for a few hours, the humming already seems out of place. They flock toward the rear exit to see who the newcomer is.

Sitting on a black and green four-wheeler is Colton, Heather's farming husband. He whips his head around, looking panicked in all directions then hops off the ATV, leaving it running, and pushes the clinic's back door open. Officer Chase does his song and dance of holding his gun in Colton's face, but Will quickly puts his hand on the barrel and lowers it.

"What are you all doing standing around in here?" Colton asks with wide eyes and trembling hands. "Don't you know the world's gone crazy?"

"If the world's so crazy what are you doing driving around in it on a four-wheeler?" Will responds, holding his other arm out blocking Heather's advances. Her look appears agitated, but her petite frame can't push past Will, so she lets the conversation continue.

Colton shuffles forward, reaching for Heather. "I'm here for my wife. I had to drive that thing"—he points outside to his ride—"because the psychopaths running around ruined my truck. They tore out the gas line, so when I tried to start it, all I got was sputtering." *So they didn't just ruin our vehicles?*

Will lowers his arm and lets Heather pass. She immediately runs into Colton who doesn't open his arms to her until she's already holding him. Even then, his motions seem stiff. His black button-up has darker stains. *Probably from the gas.*

In the woods behind the office, two boxers appear from the trees. "Your four-wheeler is making too much noise. You need to shut it off and get back in here quickly," Will orders.

"We aren't staying holed up here. I'm taking Heather away from this." Colton half-shields Heather from Will, almost defensively. *Will Daniel try to come after me too? Is he alive? Is Lucas?*

"But where will you go?" Officer Chase tries to reason. "As far as I can tell, this could be happening everywhere."

Colton backs up like an injured dog. "Doesn't matter." He nudges Heather to open the door. Once she does, they both slip through it and straddle his ATV. As he squeezes the gas, the dogs who are only feet from him pick up their pace. Colton pulls away from the clinic and his pursuers sprint in an effort to catch him. The staff lose sight of them once they round the corner of the building. The sound of his engine grows distant.

"I guess I should take advantage of this opportunity," Will says, opening the back door.

Officer Chase grabs his arm. "What do you think you're doing?"

"All the ones close enough to hear the four-wheeler just went chasing after it. In the farm call truck right outside this door is a pistol and a tranquilizer gun. Two more forms of protection. If they find a way in, we don't stand a chance with one gun and a couple shovels."

The cop appears to think about this for a moment then releases Will and nods. Both men slip out the door while the rest watch, scanning the woods for any signs of movement. Will pulls on the handle of the driver's door and hops into the seat. His body bends toward the passenger side as he rummages, then he slides out of the truck brandishing a pistol. Leaving the door open, he moves to the enclosed customized bed cap designed to hold and conceal medicine bottles, syringes, blood tubes, and everything else needed for farm and house calls.

He drops the tailgate down softly and lifts the lockable hatch. He eases the long tranquilizer rifle out and looks around anxiously. Will closes the hatch and tailgate and as he walks back to the building, he pushes the driver's door closed. It slams shut louder than he means for it to and Officer Chase twists around, on alert, for anything that might have heard it.

Four people appear at the wood's edge and run down the bank toward the two men. Blood drips from bite marks and soaks their ripped clothing. Two small breed dogs come around the corner, bodies trembling. Officer Chase aims his gun at the closest one but doesn't fire. He shoves Will toward the building without turning away. Walking backward, he fills the gap between him and the door, but the drooling, stumbling pursuers close in. Will gets inside the door and Erin throws her arms around him. He turns back to watch the officer creep his way closer to the door. Mason holds it open for him and as soon as he's in, shuts it, twisting the bolt to lock it.

The people and dogs outside reach the door, banging and scratching on the glass. Officer Chase shuttles everyone away, out of sight of the attackers. *How long before they find a way in?*

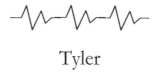

Tyler

As the sun sets, everyone gathers bedding for the long night. They take the dog cushions from the kennels for pillows and grab a few of the dozens of donated blankets to make beds on the floor. Tyler strategically works his way to the middle of the group next to Sara. The sick continue to beat against the back door.

Sara lays down on her bed and faces Tyler. The orange glow sets a fire in her hazel eyes that are still wet with tears. Tyler reaches his hand out to hold hers. "I'm sure Mila's okay. You have a great babysitter."

Sara's hand is limp, her voice is hollow when she speaks. "How could one woman protect five small children against those things?" She starts to roll away from Tyler, but he catches her shoulder, feeling brave. *Great timing.*

"Maybe they didn't attack her house. Maybe she heard the news and locked all of them up before anyone could get in. Maybe an officer was nearby and rescued them all and they're safe. You don't know, Sara." Tyler puts his hand to her cheek.

Sara sighs and continues to roll over. "Maybe

you're right, but you don't know either."

Tyler turns on his back and stares at the ceiling. Sara always does this. Her words scream for help, but when he tries to give it, she shuts him out. She wants Carter to swoop in and rescue her. But why? He doesn't seem even remotely interested in her. He's always brushing off her advances. *But I'm right here for you, Sara.*

Muffled yells coming from the closed office door pull him from his thoughts. The door swings open, revealing a red-faced Erin. She gestures for Officer Chase to leave the room. "You're as sick as those things outside if you think we're doing that!"

"Ma'am, you have to think about this rationally—"

"Rationally? What you're proposing isn't even moral, let alone rational!" Erin turns her back and looks at Will for support.

By now, the rest of the group is sitting up and watching as the argument unfolds. "What's going on?" Mason rises to his feet, looking for a potential threat.

"This sorry excuse for an officer is suggesting we *toss out* Chris, Melissa, Susan, and Carla." Erin's fury hardens her face.

"Why?" Olivia's voice raises an extra octave, and she pulls her blanket tighter around herself.

Officer Chase turns to face the makeshift beds. "Because those things out there can smell their blood, and they are going to start trying to get in even more than they already are. Not to mention the bodies are going to start to stink. And what happens if one of them changes and tries to kill any of us? Could you shoot them?"

"What do you mean change? They're dead." Erin

stares incredulously at the man.

"I watched an officer put three bullets in the chest of a man. He flinched at the impact but kept coming. They're not normal deaths, and as much as I don't want to believe it, I don't think we can take the risk that they're actually dead. There's real lives here at stake." The officer's eyes are dark.

Erin opens her mouth to protest again, but Will speaks first. "He's right." He walks into his office and emerges with a keyring. "We can move the bodies to the horse trailer. They'll be out of the clinic and away from anything wanting to chew on them."

"You can't be serious?" Erin stares at her husband in disbelief.

"Erin, we don't know how long we're going to be stuck here, but by the sounds of it, it could be a while. We have to do something with the bodies, and at least this way, there's some respect." Will waits for her to nod before addressing the rest of us. "Come on everyone, let's have a funeral."

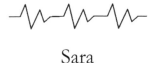

Sara

Stepping into the lobby for the second time feels wrong. It's like a forbidden place everyone is told not to go. Sara bites the scream in her throat this time. It's dark, except for the last bit of sunlight slipping behind the far-off mountains. Chairs are strewn around, and the potted plant from the corner is upset, its dirt scattered across the floor. The viewing window looking into the grooming room is busted.

Then there's the bodies.

The receptionists lay in puddles of their own blood with their empty eyes wide with the terror they died facing. Sara tries to swallow the sobs clawing their way up her throat. She hears a few others start to cry.

There are other bodies mixed in with the receptionists. With tattered clothes and gaping wounds, some clients and other people she doesn't recognize stare with those same haunting eyes. *What made them do this?* There's multiple dogs too, all with bullet holes.

Will props the front doors open while Officer Chase scans the darkness with his gun. Everyone files in toward the warmth of each other's closeness. Sara inches closer to Carter and reaches for his hand. To her surprise, his fingers interlock with hers.

Will grabs Chris's lifeless body under the arms and begins to drag him out the door toward the horse trailer off to the right of the clinic. The tears start to fall down Sara's face. When she found out she was pregnant with Mila, she had nothing. No baby clothes, no partner to help raise her, and no idea how to take care of a baby. Chris had worked with his church to get her the necessities, and Melissa and Susan had taught her how to be a mother. *How can we just dump their bodies and leave nothing to remember that?*

Before Will gets too far, Sara reaches out and puts her hand on his arm. "Wait!" Everyone's eyes fall on her. "I think we should keep something from them. Something to remember them while we're stuck here."

Silence stretches on uncomfortably. Sara feels her cheeks flush.

Erin nods. "That's a beautiful idea, Sara. What should we keep?"

Sara stoops down and looks at Chris. Today he sports a brown checked shirt with tan dress pants. Holes in the thin fabric reveal gashes in his legs. His glasses sit askew. Sara slides them from his face, folds them, and puts them in his shirt pocket. Hanging out of his pants pocket are his keys. The letters WWJD are bright yellow against the blue lanyard. The bundle of keys intermixed with keychains jingle as Sara pulls them free from his pocket.

She then stands and moves to Susan. She has a large scratch down her wrinkled face just barely missing her left eye. On her head sits a butterfly clip. Sara unlatches it from her salt and pepper hair that's matted with dried blood.

Melissa slumps against the wall, her skull bashed in. Sara tries not to look. Instead she lets her eyes travel Melissa's body until they stop on her locket. She unhooks the clasp and slides the metal from around the woman's neck. Inside are pictures of her two daughters. *Are they still alive?*

Carla is still in the grooming room. Up her right arm run a series of bite marks. The large black dog that bit her lays to the side with a bullet hole in the back of its head. In the darkness, Sara's eyes catch a glimpse of something shiny. She reaches for Carla's left hand and runs her thumb over her new engagement ring. A lump forms in her throat as she slides it from Carla's finger.

Sara rejoins the group and lets the men carry the bodies. *What if we're rescued tomorrow?* The receptionists, Carla, and the clients are taken to the horse trailer while the dogs and other mangled corpses are left outside around the side of the building.

Sara's mental image of the impromptu funeral

included all of them sharing fond memories of the coworkers, but too soon, the paranoia of the darkness pushes them back further and further until they're in the treatment area again.

On the counter in pharmacy, Sara spreads out the trinkets. These are all they have from their coworkers until they get out of here. *If we get out of here.* Sara shakes her head, feeling the weight of death crush her fragile optimistic moment.

She tucks herself back into bed, letting her heavy eyes droop until they finally close. The dying adrenaline from today allows sleep to pull her under. In her last conscious thoughts, she whispers goodbye to Mila.

Chapter Five

Day two
Sydney

In the early hours of the morning, Sydney rolls onto her back, stiff from last night on the hard ground and the lack of sleep. Beside her, Carter lays awake, so she turns to face him. "Do you think it's this bad everywhere?" She whispers, trying not to arouse anyone who may be achieving sleep.

You're thinking about Spencer, aren't you?" he asks, his voice as soft as the hand he lays on hers.

Sydney nods, ashamed of seeming so selfish. Will and Erin, Sara, and Lynn all have kids, and everyone here has family in unknown situations. *But Spencer is mine.* She lets the tears form in her eyes but refuses to let them fall. "At least we're all friends here. We can take care of each other." She hopes her words lighten the mood.

"I'm afraid being this close will make tensions start to rise. I think Sara is trying to get closer to me, and I don't want to hurt her." His face flushes bright red.

Sydney squeezes his hand. "I think you need to be upfront and honest with her, but remember grief can make one crazy. She's worried about Mila and probably desperate for someone to be close to. You know she's always had a thing for you."

"I know. That's what I'm worried about. If I tell her I'm not interested, will that break her even more?"

"Carter, you can't make yourself not gay, and you can't keep pretending there's a chance forever." She tries to level him a look, but her heart aches. They've been friends since she moved here, and he confided in her about his sexuality and how he was judged and bullied all through school. "The whole world can't be like this. Help is coming. Once we're out of these tight quarters, she will be okay again."

"It's too late for us." Sara's flat voice breaks the silence, louder than our quiet conversation. I shoot a look at Carter. *How much of that did she hear?*

"Don't say that Sara, we'll get out of here soon." Erin sits propped up against the wall, draped in a thin green blanket.

Sara sits up. "So what if we get out of here? We have supplies here, sure, but only two guns. All of us aren't going to make it with two guns, and our people on the outside will be dead. So what's the point in surviving?"

"Sara, don't you want to get out of here to see Mila again?" Lynn reaches her arm out to comfort her, but Sara jerks away.

"Didn't you hear me? They'll be dead. Mila, Lucas, Spencer, everyone we know. They were alone and defenseless and they're dead." Her cold stare freezes any words of argument. *Is she right? Spencer is my savior, my safe haven. He can't be dead. I will get back to him.*

"We can get more guns," Tyler says. "We can fight our way out of here and to our families before they're gone." He sends a quick glance to Sara.

"Where will we get guns?" Olivia asks, sounding unconvinced.

"I have one in my car, and I think Lynn does too." Tyler looks to Lynn who nods before he continues. "And what's right over the hill?"

Understanding comes to Sydney. "The police station!"

"Exactly. They have guns, ammo, and maybe another way to reach help. Right Officer Chase?"

Everyone looks at the policeman who appears caught off guard by being interrogated. He recomposes himself. "There are guns and ammo. There's also a long-range battery-operated radio we can use to call for help. I know the whole town is calling for help, but maybe as a fighting force we could end all of this."

"Then what are we waiting for?" Tiffany asks, grabbing the shovel in the corner. "Let's smash some zombie piñatas!"

Erin shakes her head. "All of us can't go. This place has medical supplies, food, and water. If we all leave, we risk it becoming overrun by those things."

"Then we split into two groups. One to stay here and protect the building, and one to gather supplies from the police station." Will scans over everyone like he's weighing the odds of who would be best sent.

"I'll lead the group to the station. I know where everything is, and I have the keys to get in. I should only need three or four." Officer Chase walks to the back door and looks toward the police station then turns back to the huddled group. "Who wants to go?"

Mason is the first to raise his hand. "I'll go to protect against the dogs." He doesn't elaborate further, but no one pushes him. He doesn't talk about his time in the military much, but he has said on multiple occasions he would die before killing another human.

Sydney surprises herself when she cautiously lifts her hand just high enough for Officer Chase to see and nod in her direction.

"I'll gladly take some fresh air." Olivia steps forward next to Tiffany, who is still brandishing her shovel.

"I want to go too. I need to feel like I'm doing something." Carter joins the small huddle.

"Alright, five it is." Officer Chase levels a stare at each of them. "But this isn't a game. It's literally life or death out there. Those people don't listen to reason or care if you beg or cry. Always stick with the group and watch each other's backs, and above all else, stay quiet. Sound attracts them."

Everyone picks up something to defend themselves with whether it's a shovel or a mere broom handle. After Mason grabs a sharp knife from the staff room, they slip out the back door.

Tiffany

It's only been about twenty-four hours since Tiffany's been outside, but it feels longer. The morning sun warms her skin, and the quiet masks the current situation with a false serenity. The police station sits over the hill. She can make out the black roof a short distance away. She steals a glance at the empty surroundings. The road off to her left sits quiet. *How did the world come to a halt so quickly?*

In the gravel parking lot of the police station, three police vans sit on one end while two other vehicles sit on the other. Below each one is a circle of darkened gravel. Officer Chase approaches one and picks up a few rocks, bringing them close to his face. "Gasoline," he whispers. "The lines are busted."

Tiffany and Carter exchange a quick glance of fear before the group starts moving again. At the front door, Officer Chase slips a key ring out of his pocket and sifts through them before selecting the right one. The bolt turns with a click and they all file into the dark building. With only a few windows, Tiffany wonders how they'll be able to find anything. At the front desk, Officer Chase pulls open a drawer, revealing two flashlights. He gives one to Mason and one to Tiffany. He pulls his own from his belt and shines it down a hallway lined with doors.

The techs follow the cop to the first door. He unlocks it and points to Mason, Olivia, and Carter. "You three go in here, it's our break room. Fill the backpacks and lunchboxes with all the food and bottled water you can. We have a lot of mouths to feed. We will be right down this hall. If you hear anything, you come find me immediately." He turns away before they have a chance to argue—not that Tiffany thought they would.

Tiffany and Sydney follow Officer Chase past three more doors that look like offices. When he gets to the one he wants, he unlocks it and they step in. The room holds two desks, a holding cell, and a large gun safe. Tiffany inwardly shudders as the memory of being in a small cold cell like this one enters her mind. She was 26 and so strung out, she thought she was in a zoo. Brent had given her name up in order to save himself. *Why did I go back to him?*

On one desk sits a radio box bolted to the desk and a few handhelds on their charging station. Officer Chase puts two handhelds in his pocket and dials the combination to the safe and opens it to reveal an assortment of pistols and rifles. He grabs a duffle bag from under one of the desks and tosses it to Tiffany. "You two load all the guns and ammo into this." He turns to the radios.

As he tries to reach other police forces on the larger box radio, Tiffany and Sydney pull guns off their racks and place them in the bag. Tiffany takes one of the pistols and sticks it in the waistband of the back of her pants. *This might come in handy. Maybe now I can keep Brent off my case.* She gestures for Sydney to do the same, but she shakes her head.

A loud crash from down the hall freezes their movements. Officer Chase holds up a hand for them to stay still as he inches toward the door. He looks down the hall then disappears around the corner. With all the guns in the bag, Tiffany grabs a strap. "Help me carry this."

Sydney hesitates. "He told us to stay here."

Tiffany rolls her eyes. "He also said to stick with

the group, so let's find the others before the zombies find us." Sydney shudder but Tiffany feels relief as the other girl grabs the opposite strap on the overstuffed duffle bag. They carry the heavy bundle between them and inch down the hall.

Back in the break room sits a small round table with four folding chairs. A countertop lines two walls along with an older model refrigerator. A shattered glass jar of what looks like salsa covers the grey and black tiled floor. The three techs hoist several bags onto their shoulders full of bottled drinks and canned foods.

"Where's Officer Chase?" Tiffany asks, reaching one hand to her backside but not revealing her weapon.

Mason slides past them into the hallway. "He went to the front to see if the noise had alerted anyone. We have everything we can carry, so let's go meet up with him."

They fall behind him in a quiet parade back to the main room. When they step outside, they still don't see their leader. A gurgling noise comes from around the corner, followed by a grunt of effort. They follow the sounds and watch as Officer Chase wrestles with one of the sick. It's a woman, maybe in her thirties, wearing a police uniform. Her blonde hair hangs in a loose bun falling into her face. Blood drenches her clothes and bare arms. A circular bite mark stands out on her neck.

Officer Chase pulls a knife from his belt and stabs it into the chest of his attacker. The fresh blood soaks her clothes but her advances don't falter. *That should have killed her. Or at least made her stop.* Tiffany instinctively reaches her hand to her stomach where a scar is the reminder of a drug deal gone wrong. The pain of a knife pushed into her gut is insanely sobering.

Tiffany stops daydreaming and joins in, swinging her shovel wide. The blade embeds itself into the woman's neck, sending more spurts of blood. She staggers back a few steps but springs forward again, teeth clamping together repeatedly. Tiffany pulls on the shovel handle trying to retrieve her weapon. Officer Chase stares at the woman, looking for a weak point. "Dammit, Marlene," he says through gritted teeth. "Why won't you stop?"

Olivia sets her food bags down and reaches for the guns. She pulls out a small pistol, checks to see if it has bullets, then aims it at the woman's head. Officer Chase glances in her direction but it's too late. His "No" is lost in the sharp pop of Olivia's gunshot.

The woman crumples to the ground, a bullet hole in the center of her forehead. Olivia momentarily looks proud of herself until Officer Chase quick steps to stand right in front of her. "What did I say? Sound attracts them. Dozens of them will be here any minute." His disapproval is clear with every word. He turns to address the rest of the group. "Grab all the bags and move. We don't have much time." He picks up the bag of guns and slings it over his shoulder. Everyone else grabs the food bags and falls into a jog behind him.

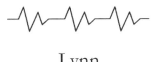

Lynn

With Officer Chase's group gone, Lynn and Tyler rummage through the staff cars looking for weapons.

Lynn collects all the bottles of perfume, deciding they'll be helpful until they can get out of here and shower.

In her blue Traverse, Lynn opens the center console and pulls out her small 9mm. She looks at the gun, thinking about how many times she thought about using it. On Daniel. On herself. She knows the thoughts are dark and she always dismisses them, but they still exist. Also, in her car is her bottle of antidepressants. Daniel doesn't know about them, since he'd probably be against them for some reason or another, so she keeps the bottle in her car.

Tyler rejoins her with his arms loaded with supplies. He has a few pistols, a baseball bat, and several packs of gum.

The loud crack of a gunshot makes Lynn jump and she nearly drops the bottle of medicine. "Where did that come from?"

Tyler looks around then nods toward the door. "I don't know, but it sounded close. Let's get inside before something comes to investigate."

"Wait. This is our opportunity to try our cars. The gunshot was loud enough to attract any nearby threats, right?" Lynn removes a bundle of keys from her pocket. She had been hoping for this chance.

"I'm not sure that's a good idea…" But he doesn't try to stop her.

Lynn slides into her driver's seat and sticks her key in the ignition. As she turns it, the engine sputters. She twists on it again, harder.

"All your gas is spraying on the ground. Come on, let's go. Tyler's voice is panicked.

Lynn removes her key. This was her chance to take off and never look back. And it failed.

Carter

Strolling downhill to the police station was easy, but attempting to jog back uphill with a loaded bag burns Carter's calves. Stopping to readjust the backpack falling off his shoulders, he steals a glance from where they came and feels his heart rate skyrocket. At least a dozen dogs and half a dozen awkward fumbling zombies have reached the base of the hill they're climbing. "Chase!" he calls out. *Too late to worry about being quiet.*

The officer whips his head around, probably to shush him, but sees the bad scenario unfolding. He slides back down the hill to where Carter stands and drops his gun bag. "Arm yourselves," he orders as he aims his own gun.

"What about the noise?" Olivia asks spitefully.

"Right now, we're outnumbered. If you want to continue taking jabs at my leadership, you will wind up getting yourself killed. Now everyone, start walking backwards but protect yourselves and each other." Officer Chase picks up what's left of the gun stash and puts it back on his shoulder. A tall wolfhound comes at him, quickly filling in the safety cushion of space. He fires his pistol, knocking his attacker's head back with the bullet.

Carter aims a rifle at a short man running toward the cop. He pulls the trigger and watches the figure fall. Gunshots fill the air, and he can only imagine what the group back at the clinic must be thinking. Tiffany,

Mason, and Olivia all have pistols, while Officer Chase brandishes a rifle.

To his right, Carter notices Sydney staring at the small silver pistol in her hands. She flips it over as the uncertainty becomes clear on her face. Carter works his way to her, to comfort her, but something black catches his eye.

A black pit bull barrels toward Sydney, and she sees it. Her hand movements freeze, and her legs visibly begin to tremble. Carter can almost feel her fear radiating, and he hurls his body in front of hers. The terrier barrels into him, knocking him off his feet as a sharp pain shoots up his side. *Was that claws or teeth?* A gunshot goes off, and a Carter feels an impact connect with the beast assaulting him. It goes limp, and he pushes it away. He shifts his backpack to hide the blood soaking his scrub top, grabs Sydney's hand, and quickly climbs the hill to the rest of the group. Three more dogs come from the parking lot, leaving them sandwiched between the two forces.

Carter releases Sydney's hand to tighten both of his on his gun. Olivia sidles in close to them. Before they can react, Olivia and Carter are both grabbed. Carter yells but twists away from his attacker and knocks the scraggly haired man in the head with the butt of his gun. Olivia continues to struggle. Before Carter can shoot, the man trips Olivia and once she falls, he claws her midsection, tearing clothing and flesh. Her screams ring louder than the gunshots. Carter's eyes feel as though they are going to pop out of his head, but he can't look away. The zombie gnaws at her insides, covering his face with her blood. Olivia's blank eyes and mouth lay open, staring at him in shock and accusation for being unable to save her in time.

Carter lands another head shot and the zombie falls on top of Olivia. Sydney pulls at his arm. He forces himself to sprint along with her. His labored breath and sobs intermix. *This just can't be real.* Officer Chase continues to push the group back and the glass door of the building comes into view. Sydney is the first to reach it and she flings it open. They all pile in with Officer Chase being the last. He slams the door, locking it, and motions for everyone to move away further.

Once out of sight, they all let out a breath of relief. The clawing and banging on the door soon follow.

The group that stayed behind take the bags and begin sorting the supplies where it needs to go while the others collect themselves from the fight. Finally, Erin notices. "Where's Olivia?"

Officer Chase only shakes his head. Erin places her hand over her mouth and her eyes glisten with a new wetness.

Chapter Six

Day four
Lynn

"I still can't believe she's actually gone," Lynn says in a quiet voice. "I should have been nicer to her." She is patrolling around the outside of the clinic with Mason. He carries a shovel, a large butcher knife and pistol strapped to his waist. Lynn holds her pistol in one hand and Jake's leash in the other. The three-legged pup hobbles along, clueless to the world falling apart around him. Despite all the fear and heartache, Lynn feels happier in this moment than she has in a long time.

"Lynn, you're one of the nicest people I know. I'm sure Olivia thought the same," Mason reassures her. "Maybe I could have saved her if I could bring myself to shoot these things. It's strange. I'm a vet tech but don't have any problem shooting the dogs, because inside, I know they're not themselves anymore, but the people… I just can't reach that same conclusion." He turns away, appearing ashamed.

Lynn stops walking and places her hand on Mason's arm. "I don't think that makes you strange. It means you care about what happens to those people, even if they're not people anymore. I know you've seen too much killing in your life already, and no one can hold that against you. I also know you'll protect us more than any other person if the dogs attack."

Mason looks at Lynn and she feels like for the first time he's really seeing her. He lifts a hand to place on her cheek. "I would protect you from anything. Say the word and it's done."

Tears spring to Lynn's eyes. She battles with herself about telling Mason everything about Daniel. When they get out of this, he could take her away from all that. They could be together. But if this is their life now, and Daniel is already dead, why ruin the moment by bringing him up?

She stuffs the debate away for another time. Right now, she enjoys being and nothing more.

"You two should bring Jake inside, something's happening." Tyler pokes his head out the backdoor and breaks the fragile moment.

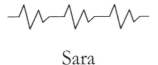

Sara

Sara stands at the end of the run hallway watching as Will, Erin, and Officer Chase try to loop a catch pole around a dog's head. The two dogs boarding in the runs have become more aggressive with each day. No one can even take them for walks anymore, and they're uninterested in the dog food slid underneath the door.

"If you just hold it long enough for me to open the cage door, I could sedate it," Will says through clinched teeth. He aims his tranquilizer gun.

Officer Chase has the door cracked enough to fit the pole through and he tries maneuvering the loop around the dog. "What do you think I'm trying to do?" The whole time, Finn snarls and snaps at the pole when it gets too close.

"What's going on?" Tyler asks from behind Sara.

"I think they're euthanizing Finn and Chance," she replies, sparing Tyler only a glance.

"What about Jake? Where is he?" Tyler looks toward the open kennel door in the treatment area.

"Lynn and Mason took it for a walk," she says without much emotion.

Tyler walks away, and Sara turns back to the runs. Officer Chase successfully loops the dog and flings the door open. Will takes the shot, and the dog wobbles for a few moments before slumping to the floor. Cautiously, Erin walks into the large kennel and administers euthanasia solution into the dog's vein. They repeat the procedure with Chance in the next run then turn to leave the hallway.

Lynn and Mason stand in the middle of the treatment area with Jake. Officer Chase nods in their direction. "We should probably do that one too while he's still touchable."

Lynn gasps and tightens her hold on the leash, but it's Sydney's outburst that catches everyone off guard.

"No! You won't touch him!" She moves to stand between the dog and the officer.

"Look, Sydney, I don't like this anymore than you do, but what if the dog turns and escapes his cage? That puts us all at risk." Officer Chase tries to reason.

Sara nods along to the officer's words. *That's a good point.*

"What if he's never going to turn and you're killing him for no reason? I don't see you going after Josie?"

"I haven't seen this affect cats, so she's less of a threat right now, but I have seen it affect dogs. I'm trying to keep the group safety as number one priority."

Sara finds herself enlightened by Officer Chase's words. Maybe she couldn't save Mila, and that's a pain she'll have to deal with one day, but she could protect this group. She could protect Carter.

"I've seen it affect dogs and people. Are you going to start euthanizing us because we *might* turn?" Sydney's anger seems to surprise everyone, evident by their wide eyes and gapping mouths.

Officer Chase clamps his mouth shut and levels a hard stare at Sydney. "Fine. But at the first sign of him turning, I'll put him down myself." He turns away and the onlookers begin to dissipate.

Tyler appears at Sara's side and she lets out a sigh of annoyance. "That was more excitement than I've seen for two days. How about you?"

Sara ignores his question. "Did you see where Carter went?"

A pained look crosses Tyler's face but Sara doesn't acknowledge it. "I think he went up front with Sydney," Tyler mumbles.

Why does he spend so much time with Sydney?

Carter

Carter dips his scrub brush in the soapy cold mop water again and sets to cleaning the next tile on the floor in reception. The bodies may be gone, but the smell of blood is strengthening. Carter feels like it's clinging to the inside of his nose. It's all he can smell.

As he bends his body to reach a blood splatter, a sharp pain shoots up his side. He puts his hand against the wound he earned on the trip to the police station. *I'm going to need more Ibuprofen soon.*

One of the doors from the treatment area open and Carter turns around to see who it is. Sydney walks to where he is and sinks to her knees beside him. She brandishes her own scrub brush and silently sets to work helping him erase the evidence of their friends' deaths.

After several minutes, she finally breaks the silence. "They wanted to euthanize Jake."

"What?" Carter stops to look at her. "Why?"

Tears fill Sydney's eyes. Carter takes her hand and she cries until no more tears come. Carter can see the weight of everything's that's happened the past few days drowning her. As she begins to catch her breath and calm down, her confession falls from her mouth. "I was afraid of Jake. Pit bulls in general make me nervous, but especially Jake. I was in reception when the man came in with him. He was scared and in pain and I ran. I hid in an exam room so I wouldn't have to take the dog to the doctors."

Carter feels shocked at what he hears. Sydney has always been so compassionate about what she does, but to make an injured dog wait longer for pain relief? That just doesn't sound like her.

"When I was younger and living with my dad, he used to raise and train fighting dogs. His favorite was a huge black pit bull named King. One night, I thought I'd be the hero and let the dogs free. I know that would mean they wouldn't have a home, but I thought that would be better than living with my dad and being made to fight. My dad caught me as King was warming up to me and in the chaos of getting me away and shutting the cage, King lunged and bit me." Sydney dissolves into sobs again.

Carter feels himself soften even more. "And Jake looks like King, so he reminds you of that night."

Sydney nods. "I'm sure you think I'm pathetic since I still let it bother me this much."

"Are you kidding? You were a kid and that had to have been traumatic. Plus, your dad doesn't sound like father of the year material, so I'm sure growing up was hard anyway. I'm amazed you're a vet tech after having that sort of experience."

Sydney sniffles. "I want to help animals. More than anything. I told Officer Chase he wasn't euthanizing Jake because there isn't anything wrong with him. I just had this urge to protect him. I couldn't save King, but I can protect Jake. I'm sure that sounds dumb, but I just have to."

"It doesn't sound dumb, Sydney." Carter gives his friend a hug. Her scent masks the blood covering the floor. She smells lightly of sweat, but she's recently used Febreze to freshen her scent. Her hair has a faint whiff of her shampoo still lingering. *Why are all these scents so strong?*

The door opens again and the two break apart and look toward the sound. Tyler stomps his way in their direction.

"What is it with you?" he demands, pointing at Carter.

"What are you talking about?" Carter puts a hand on the reception desk and pulls himself to his feet. Sydney stands up too but shies away from the confrontation.

"You have the undying attention of the most perfect girl and you don't even give her a second glance. You'd rather be out here seducing a girl who is already in a committed relationship." Tyler's face is red from trying to keep his voice low and even.

"Seducing? I was comforting my friend. I'm not interested in Sydney like that." Carter puts his hands out in a calm down gesture.

"Don't give me that. Ever since you started working here, you've thrown off everything."

"Seriously, what is your problem? If you like Sara, then tell her. That has nothing to do with me."

"It has everything to do with you! She's in love with you and you act like you can't see it!" Tyler's fists clench at his sides. Sydney's eyes dart between the two, unsure of what to do.

"I know Sara likes me, and I'm sorry that's causing her to overlook your own affection, but I can assure you I'm not in competition with you."

"Oh yeah? And why's that?" Tyler asks, raising an eyebrow.

Carter shoots Sydney a look and watches her eyes

grow before he takes a deep breath. "I'm not interested in Sara because I'm gay."

"You're… what?" Tyler's anger falters.

Carter gives a silent nod. Sydney was the only person here who knew the truth. Carter grew up being bullied about his sexuality by friends, schoolmates, and even family. He needed a fresh start and taking a job here, ten hours away from his old home gave him that. He didn't plan on telling anyone the truth unless he felt they would accept him. Now here he was, telling someone who looked like they were just about to punch him.

Tyler's shoulders slump as his muscles relax. He doesn't reply. He just turns away and goes back through the door to the treatment area.

Carter sinks back to the floor and begins scrubbing again. Anger boils in his chest, a rage so strong and foreign to him. He wanted the fight to happen. He wanted to dominate Tyler and show him what kind of threat he really was.

But not yet.

"Carter…" Sydney's soft voice pulls him out of his thoughts.

"Drop it." His clipped response has the desired effect and Sydney stays quiet as they continue scrubbing the floor.

Tiffany

Tiffany walks into the staff room to check her pill bottle again. *I have to stop doing this before someone sees me.*

Olivia's death was more than a shock to everyone. Yes, other people died, but she saw Olivia being torn to shreds. The images haunted Tiffany's dreams the past two nights. *What could I have done differently to save her?* Taking a pill or two and dipping out for a while doesn't sound like a bad idea, but Tiffany knows she can't. Once she starts, she won't quit.

Sara sits on the couch in the staff room, and the sight of her makes Tiffany freeze. *Is she waiting for me because she knows?* Tiffany dismisses the paranoid thought and plops down next to her friend. "Hey, what's up?"

"Nothing. I just have a lot on my mind, so I came in here to think." Sara picks at a loose thread on the drawstrings of her scrub pants.

"Don't we all? Want to talk about it?" Tiffany curls her feet under her and turns to her side to face Sara like the hundreds of nights they've spent together talking about everything under the sun from school, to work, to boys, to family. One night, she even broke down and confided in Sara everything about her life on drugs. Sara never once judged, and their friendship only grew from that point.

"What's the hardest thing you would do to protect everyone here?" Sara levels a serious look at Tiffany, catching her off guard.

"Wow, um… I don't really know."

"Would you kill one of us if you had to?"

Again, Tiffany is stunned by Sara's question. "I mean, I guess if one of us turns and there's no other choice. That's probably not something anyone could answer until it happens."

"I think I could. If it meant protecting the people I

love." Sara turns away and returns her focus to her string.

Tiffany sits quietly for a little while longer before rising to leave. She reminds herself that Sara is grieving for Mila, however strange her process is seeming.

Chapter Seven

Day seven
Tyler

"I just want to know how long we're going to be here," Tiffany states over dinner of canned chicken and corn. Tyler's stomach rumbles at the small portion of food. He knows they have to stretch their resources, but he could really go for an all-you-can-eat buffet.

"That's the big question we all wished we had an answer to," Officer Chase says through bites of food.

"I've got an even bigger question for you all." Tyler tries his best to force back his smile.

"What's that?" Erin asks curiously.

Tyler sets his plate down and swings his arms in a small dance as he sings, "Who let the dogs out? Woof. Woof. Woof. Woof." To his amazement, no one laughs.

Officer Chase levels him a hard stare. "Do you

think this situation is funny? Do the deaths of your coworkers mean nothing to you? Is this all just a big joke?"

Tyler's shoulder's turn in. "I just thought, with all the sadness, a joke would be good for everyone."

"Well, no one's laughing, are they?"

Tyler stands and walks away from the group. He wasn't trying to upset anyone. What could he do to make it up to them? He soon finds himself in pharmacy. It's been a few days since the trip to the police station and Olivia's death. Josie leaps up onto the counter demanding attention. He strokes her white and brown fur allowing himself to get lost in thought. His eyes travel to the keepsakes. The idea strikes him. He knows what everyone really needs.

Tyler slips through the pharmacy door into the lobby. He walks across the white-tiled floor now free of blood splatters, the only evidence of what happened on the first day everything changed. A few days ago, Sydney and Carter used cold mop water and brushes to scrub the stains away. They scrubbed furiously, as if they could erase what happened as easily as the morbid paint job. That is, until he interrupted them.

He never suspected Carter was gay. He doesn't know how to feel about it. He doesn't have a problem with gay people, but why doesn't' Carter tell Sara so she'll stop obsessing over him? Maybe he's not really gay. But why lie? Tyler shakes his head, shoving back the thoughts. *I can win Sara's heart regardless of Carter.*

Tyler sneaks out the front door of the clinic and clings to the wall of the building, his back rubbing against the textured bricks, until he decides he doesn't see or hear anyone. *I just have to make it to the hill.* The air outside doesn't smell fresh anymore. There's too much death. The humming of the flies over the corpses is loud enough to sound like a car rumbling down the road.

The sun setting amidst the twilight haze, Tyler looks closely at the bodies to make out who or what they are. Finally, he comes across the one he wants. There's not much left on Olivia's bones. A lot of the skin and muscle has been stripped away by the zombies. He searches the area until he finds what he came for. The blue hair scrunchie she always wore on her wrist lays a few feet away. *I don't want to know where the red one is.*

Once the prize is in his possession, Tyler dashes back up the hill. Before he gets too close, he watches three large dogs sprint toward the front door. He drops down onto his belly and tries to make himself invisible in the not-high-enough grass. It's getting too dark to make out the breed, but Tyler can tell the dogs aren't coming for him. He watches as they drop items from their mouth onto the sidewalk directly in front of the main door. *What the hell?*

Tyler crawls in his prone position, heading for the back door. The tense, slow progression causes sweat to flow down his back. Every few seconds he looks over his shoulder. At the door, he pulls himself to his feet, but rams a pointy stick into his arm. The twig penetrates enough for a couple droplets of blood to dot the ground under him, but he pulls it out and tosses it away.

Inside the building, Tyler is immediately confronted by Officer Chase and Will. "Where have you been? You can't just run off like that." Will's face is red with anger.

"I know, but I had to get this." Tyler produces the scrunchie. "I thought it would help with some closure." He walks over to where Sara stands and holds out the keepsake.

She looks at it without really seeing it then walks away. Tyler's heart sinks. *Why doesn't she care?*

Will lectures Tyler on being smart and keeping the group's safety in mind, but then goes back to his office. Tyler goes to the pharmacy to add the scrunchie to the rest of the trinkets.

Everything is becoming so weird. With only ten of them trapped here, he thought things would be simplistic. Meals are divided, bathroom breaks are in pairs, and everyone should become used to the idea of no secrets in these close quarters, but that's not the case. Tyler feels like the people he's been working with his friends are strangers. The confinement is changing them. Especially Sara. She's began to distance herself. Maybe if he had been there for her more in the beginning…

It's hard to believe it's only been a week. The days carry on at impossible lengths, with little to differentiate the passing time. Officer Chase hasn't heard from his partners in two days. Occasionally, dogs will bark and scratch on the back door, but no one confronts them. Everyone just hides out of sight until they leave. There must be more they could do. *We can't stay here like this forever.*

Carter interrupts Tyler's daydreaming as he rounds the corner and begins rummaging through some of the medicine bottles.

"What are you looking for?" Tyler asks, inching

closer out of curiosity.

"Some Azithromycin or something. I think my allergies are trying to take a stab at me. I'm not feeling my best."

"Maybe you should let Will or Erin know and they could prescribe something for you?"

"How do you know I didn't already? Besides, they're vets, not human doctors. No need to bother anyone, I'm not helpless." He snatches the desired bottle from the shelf and stalks away.

Tyler watches Carter's departure. *That was pretty hateful.* Tyler knows he's probably not Carter's favorite person right now, but that harshness was odd.

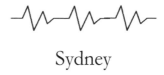

Sydney

Sydney squats down in front of Jake's kennel and stares into his eyes. *Is he going to change into one of those dogs outside?* She thinks about sticking her fingers through the bars. Just a soft touch of his fur. She lifts her hand while continuing to watch him for any signs of movement.

There's a single bark at the backdoor. Sydney has become good at blocking out the constant noises of the dogs but this one sounds different. Almost like an exclamation or an order.

The backdoor flies open with a strong force that shatters the glass. Five or six zombies pour in, followed by a mismatched pack of dogs. Sydney bolts up and swipes her hands across her body. *What did I do with my gun?* Her panic makes her freeze and feel lightheaded as if she's going to pass out.

Carter grabs Sydney's arm and shoves her into the run hallway toward the laundry room. She hears the heavy steps of the thing pursuing them.

They slam the door behind them and put their weight against it. "What if there's more than one after us?" Carter asks as the knob begins to jiggle.

"I'm going to move the washing machine, hold the door!" Sydney begins to shimmy the washer back and forth filling the gap between it and the door, stretching the water lines tight. Once the metal meets the wood, Carter lets go and moves to stand beside her behind the washer. The knob stills.

The two stare through the small window in the door. The mutilated face that stares back at them stays motionless. Claw marks leave gashes along its cheek. A large black mosquito emerges from the wound and crawls across its face, out of sight. Its glossy eyes pierce into Sydney. They're not the eyes of a predator instinctively chasing a meal, but rather intelligent eyes calculating every possibility and probability of getting into the room. Her heart pounds so hard it makes her ears hurt. She feels the heat from Carter's body pressed up against hers, his fingers intertwined with her trembling ones.

Distant gunshots break the tense moment. Carter doesn't break eye contact with the zombie but speaks very matter of factly. "They're going to get us all. One by one."

"We'll be okay. If we stick together, we'll get out of here."

"They've already made it inside. It's too late for the rest of you." Carter turns to stare into Sydney's eyes. The longing look is one she had never seen from him before.

"The rest of us?" Her voice is barely above a whisper and gets lost as Carter crushes her lips against his. Shock consumes her as he shoves her against the washer, his kiss hungry. *What is he doing?* Her mind screams as his mouth forces hers to open and his tongue snakes in skidding along her teeth. Sydney brings her hands up and pushes against his chest. She's surprised by his strength when his body doesn't budge.

When he does draw away, his teeth nips at her lips. The sharp pain makes her gasp, and when she raises her hand to the spot, it comes away with a sear of blood.

Before she has a chance to push for an explanation a louder, closer gunshot rings in her ears and the face outside the door slams into the window with a splatter of blood. The body slumps down out of sight revealing Lynn standing in the hallway with her pistol still pointed. Sydney grabs the washer and starts to move it. "Come on, let's get out of here."

Carter doesn't move. He continues to stare at Sydney until his eyes shift to focus on Lynn. "Bullets don't last forever."

"But they're working for the time being, so help me!" She shoots him a glare she hopes says, "What the hell?"

Finally, his stare breaks and he takes the other side of the washer. Together they shift it back to its original position and open the door. The corpse flops onto the floor in front of them. They step over it and rush to Lynn. "Are there more inside? Is anyone hurt?' Sydney asks, eyes flitting to the end of the hall leading back to the treatment area.

"That was the last one. Everyone's fine, other than Tiffany. She was shot." Lynn averts her eyes.

"Shot? By who? Is she dead?" Sydney's hysteria causes her voice to rise, and she temporarily forgets about Carter's kiss.

"She's fine. It was her leg. Erin's looking at it now and thinks it was only grazed."

Sydney ignores the fact she didn't answer the *who* part of her question. She rushes out into the treatment area. Tiffany sits in the tech desk chair with her black scrub pants down around her ankles while Erin kneels on one knee and holds a towel to Tiffany's thigh. "Son of a bitch!" Tiffany curses as Erin prods at the wound.

"Does anyone have battery life on their phone to use as a flashlight?" Erin asks while shooting Tiffany an exasperated look. "If you'd let me give you some Hydromorphone, this wouldn't hurt as bad."

"No! I don't want any drugs!" Tiffany's fists are clenched. Sydney isn't sure if it's out of pain or frustration.

"Honestly, Tiffany, it would only be a light sedation with pain relief. You wouldn't be missing out on anything." Erin presses further, but Tiffany rejects again. *Why would she refuse pain meds? Is she trying to look tough?* Erin shakes her head and looks back at the wound. "Will, I think you need to look at this. The graze is deep. Should we suture or staple it?"

"Suture and put a pressure bandage on it and we can reevaluate in the morning when the bleeding stops." Will calls from where he and Officer Chase drag bodies out the broken back door. None of the men are around. *Privacy for Tiffany?*

Erin nods and sets to work on bandaging Tiffany's thigh. Lynn grabs her a pack of suture, needle drivers, and forceps then holds one of the flashlights from the police station to help her see. Erin begins sowing the hole shot while Tiffany tries to hide her wincing.

Sydney wanders into the staff room in search of Carter. Her chaotic emotions come to a crescendo when she sees him crouched in the corner beside the couch. Questions swirl in her head. "What was that about?"

Carter doesn't look at her. "I'm sorry," he mumbles along with other things Sydney can't quite hear.

"Sorry? Carter, you're not acting like yourself. I'm so confused right now." Sydney takes a step closer toward her friend.

"Back off!" Carter growls.

Sydney's steps freeze. *That's not Carter.* She reaches her hand out to comfort him. "Tell me what's going on. I can help." As her hand touches his shoulder he stands up, spins around, and swaps her arms away. Before she can compose herself, Carter storms out of the staff room.

Mason walks through the doorway, interrupting her shock. "Everything okay, Sydney?" He asks, barely louder than a mumble.

"Yeah, but are you okay? Your voice sounds shaken." Sydney studies him closer and sees his hands are shaking as well.

"It was me who shot Tiffany."

Shock consumes Sydney's features for a moment before she composes herself. "But it was an accident, right?"

"Of course! After returning from the war, I never wanted to hurt anyone again, not even these things running around outside. I was aiming at a dog but when I fired, she stepped in the way." Regret floods his facial features.

Sydney reaches her hand out to place it on his arm. "At least you were trying to protect us. When I went to the police station, I did nothing. I might have been able to save Olivia, but I don't even know how to shoot a gun." She thinks about her next words. "Could you teach me?"

Mason averts his eyes but replies, "Would you like to learn?"

Sydney's nod is small, and Mason pulls his pistol from his bag on the couch. She watches his hands move to a slide button on the side of the gun. As he thumbs it the inside of the gun handle falls into his hand. "This is where your bullets are. There's fifteen in it since I loaded it after the siege." He shows Sydney the bullets numbered on the side then slips them into his pocket. "This top part of the gun slides back." He shows the motion. "And that's how you put the first bullet into the chamber to fire." He hands the gun to her to try.

Holding the gun in her right hand, Sydney is baffled by the weight compared to the size. She puts her left hand on top and pulls it back. There's a little tension but it makes the same clicking sound as when Mason did it. "Now when you load the first bullet and fire, the second one will automatically come up so you can keep firing until you're out of bullets." He hands her the magazine. "Pop this back into the bottom."

She slides the clip into the gun, using a bit of force

it locks into place. "What about a safety switch?" She asks, looking near the trigger for a button.

"Police guns typically don't have a safety switch because in the heat of a pursuit they don't want to get caught up and then forget to flip the safety off. This has a safe action. When you're holding the gun to fire and your finger is on the trigger the safety is off. It can't fire if you bump it or drop it, but it will fire if you're holding to shoot. So, if you're aiming, make sure you mean it." His brow creases with guilt again.

Sydney hands him his gun back. "Thank you for teaching me. Hopefully, this will all be over soon and it's not something I'll have to use." She prays that's the case. She never held a gun before all this. Her dad made sure they were something she should be afraid of. *Could I fire a gun at someone if I had too?* The answer isn't clear in her mind.

Sydney leaves the staff room to hover outside the office. Erin runs the numbers in her book and makes tally marks next to the remaining ten.

Will walks in with Officer Chase talking about the bodies they just disposed and the barricade covering the broken back door they created with the metal kennels. "Maybe the others will take it as a warning," Will offers.

"Aren't zombies more stupid than that?' Officer Chase asks, appearing to give into the undead theory.

"No." Erin's solid answer shocks them both into looking at her. "They're not stupid. They're smart, even the dogs. Just look what they did to the electric, the phone lines, our cars. It was all deliberate."

"If they're so smart, then why don't they open the front door and walk right in?" Will asks.

"Well the dogs still lack opposable thumbs, but it looks like the humans have very inhibited motor skills. Maybe they can't do everything, but they can think. There was probably even a reason they broke in now." The two men contemplate her words.

Sydney knocks softly on the door and interrupts their conversation. Her eyes shift from face to face. "Can I talk to you all?"

"Of course." Erin swivels her chair to face Sydney. Her face pales as Sydney shuts the door.

"I think there's something wrong with Carter."

"What do you mean?" Will asks as his eyebrows scrunch together.

Sydney shuffle from foot to foot then takes a deep breath. "I think he might be infected." She lets the weight of her words take affect before continuing. "When we were trapped in the laundry room, something changed in his behavior. He went from being afraid to having no fear, and he said weird things like 'it's too late for us' but excluded himself. He sensed they were coming because he reacted as soon as they came through the door."

Officer Chase rakes his hand through his short black hair. "It had to have happened when we went to the police station."

"That was five days ago. Why wouldn't he have told anyone he was bit?" Will's hand hardens into a fist.

"Think about what we would have to do to him." Sydney whispers the words as if she could make them less real if she says them quietly enough. *How could I even suggest that? But what else can we do?*

"Are you seriously suggesting we have to kill Carter?" Anger rises in Erin's voice. "Haven't we lost enough already? Killing those things outside is one thing for me to live with, but a living breathing human? My own employee? That's insane!"

Sydney bites her lip.

"There's another option." Officer Chase straightens his stance and reaches for the doorknob. "There's a holding cell at the police station. We can keep him there for a few days and see how he is. Maybe not everyone gets sick enough to die and come back. The building is fairly secure, and we can send someone to check on him a couple times a day."

"Last time we made a trip to the police station Olivia died. We can't risk that happening again." Erin argues.

"Last time Olivia fired a gun when there was one person in our way. That alerted the whole neighborhood. If we're smart and stay quiet, the trip will be easier."

"Why can't he just stay here? We could tie him up in another room until we know if he'll turn or not."

"Those things are strong. I don't want to find out how strong by testing them against a couple leashes and leaving the group here vulnerable. And if they're as smart as you say, what if he tries convincing us to let him go when he's about to turn? I think distancing him from the group would be best."

"How can we just evict him?" Erin squeezes her eyes shut for a moment and takes a deep breath. The need to protect those around her grows past her insecurities of the unknown.

"It will only be for a few days," says Officer Chase. "We don't know much about how this works yet, and we can't take the risk of everyone's safety if he decides to go on a killing spree. I'll even leave him a gun in case something gets in when we're not there."

Erin thinks about it for several minutes, her eyes staring out at nothing. A light knock on the door provokes her to give a single nod at the officer. He nods back then opens the door, revealing the six remaining techs huddled close, hoping to pick up details of the private conversation.

Will stands up, filling the doorway, and clears his throat. "I don't know how much of that any of you heard, but I'm here to tell you we are not trying to keep secrets. We were deciding a course of action for a situation that has been brought to us. Now that we have one, we can discuss it as a group if that's okay with everyone here?"

A few nods and mumbles of affirmation follow, but Carter's eyes shift back and forth. "You're talking about me, aren't you?" He takes a timid step backwards away from the group, shying away from the eyes watching him.

"We are, but we're not against you. We want to keep the group safe, but we also want to keep you safe, and we have a solution." Will holds his hands out and waves them in a calming gesture.

Carter backs himself in a corner. If he were a dog, Sydney could imagine his ears laid back and tail tucked. "Are you kicking me out?"

"No." Officer Chase walks toward him, cautiously placing his hand on the tech's shoulder. "We are going to have you stay in the cell at the police station, just for a few days. If you're still fine after that, then you can come back over here and the whole thing will be done with."

"I was scratched! I'm not sick!" Hysteria seeps into his voice.

"We don't know how this works. Maybe a scratch is all it takes to spread. Let's try this." Officer Chase pulls Carter forward out of his crouch. He takes small steps forward walking with the officer toward the back door. They disappear out of sight, and Sydney feels a tightness in her chest. *Are we doing the right thing?*

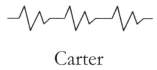

Carter

Officer Chase escorts Carter to the lobby. The moonlight shines through the door onto the clean white floor. The sight fills Carter with the memory of Sydney. Part of him aches for Sydney. To be near her. To taste her. To change her. Soon, she'll be with him.

The officer opens the door but stops. Squeaky toys, bells, and glass bottles cover the sidewalk. "What the hell?" Officer Chase shines his light around them and when he doesn't see anything, he leads Carter through the maze of noisy objects.

"It's a trap meant for us," Carter mumbles.

Officer Chase doesn't ease up on Carter's arm as they travel through the darkness toward the police station. He makes frequent sweeps with his flashlight but doesn't make mention of seeing anything.

But Carter knows they're out there watching. *Why don't you attack?*

The answer fills his mind as if coming from a thousand voices. *We don't want one. We want them all.*

"Do you really think this is the best plan?" Carter

asks aloud.

"I'm sorry, it's the best we have until we learn how this works. How do you feel? Anything weird or unusual?" The fear in the police officer's voice rings clear to Carter.

Weird or unusual? Carter fights back the dark laughter wanting to escape. "I feel fine," he lies. *Why lie?*

The voices chorus again. *Because he will kill you.*

Chapter Eight

Day nine
Sara

Sara watches out the staff room window in the direction of the police station. Her head throbs. *Just forget about him.* She tries to ignore the consuming thoughts of Carter caged up alone. She could go to him. Maybe they could run away. If they spent time together, maybe he'd start to show an interest.

But she knew she couldn't walk out of this building alone. Everyone is on red alert since the zombies broke in two days ago. Who could she trust to take with her? She knew. Someone who would do anything she asked.

Tyler stands in the pharmacy delicately touching the trinkets of the dead. He showed her the scrunchie after Olivia's death. She knew he wanted some sort of recognition, but she had none to give. What did it matter? They're dead. Just like Mila. What they need to do now is focus on keeping everyone else alive. That includes Carter.

Tyler twirls around as Sara draws closer. His shocked expression softens quickly. "Hey Sara. How are you doing?"

It's a silly question. *How are any of us really doing in all this?* The answer doesn't matter. "I need your help."

"Sure, what do you need?" His eagerness secures Sara's plan in her mind.

"It's about time someone goes to check on Carter. I want you and me to be the ones to go." Sara dismisses the disappointment darkening his eyes. She knows he wanted it to be anything other than about Carter, but if he wants her attention now, he should have stepped up before the world decided to go to hell.

"Oh, sure." Tyler walks passed her, not meeting her gaze. Sara follows him to the office where the doctors and the officer sit talking about strategies of protection. Tyler knocks lightly on the open door.

"Hey, Tyler, do you need something?" Will's voice asks lightly, but his eyes glance around for a threat.

"Sara and I wanted to let you guys know we're going to go check on Carter."

"Just the two of you? Are you sure that's safe?" Officer Chases stands as if ready to accompany them.

"We'll be okay. We're quiet, and we both know how to handle a gun," Tyler assures. A sweep of relief floods through Sara.

"I know you do, but remember you're to keep the fight quiet as long as possible before firing off a gun," Officer Chase warns.

"I also have my bat." Tyler brandishes his blunt weapon.

"Alright, don't be long. If you're not back within an hour, we're coming to look for you." Will tosses Tyler his wristwatch and a radio.

"We won't. Thanks." Tyler turns and Sara follows behind again. They slide the metal kennel away from the back door and slip through the hole in the broken glass.

The two techs creep silently down the hill. Nothing stirs around them. The sun is high in the sky, the midday warmth refreshing. How many days has it been since she's been outside longer than a bathroom break? Nine? Ten? They all seem to run together to her.

Tyler jerks his head around surveying the area, but Sara keeps her vision straight. What she wants is right in front of her, and no dogs are going to stop her.

Once inside, Tyler does a sweep through several of the rooms, but Sara rushes straight to the holding cell. It's dark with only the one high window to provide light, but she can make out his body sitting on the floor with his back to her. She tentatively takes another step forward. "Carter?"

His head swivels around with intense speed and Sara wonders how his neck didn't snap. His eyes drill into her. They're glossy, like he did some drugs, but they track her movements with a calculating look.

Sara steps closer again, the bars in front of her only an arm's length away. "Carter? Are you okay?"

"Get away Sara." His voice is strained, like he has a sore throat and it hurts to talk.

Sara flinches at his words but takes another step

forward. "I've come to check on you. Maybe we could get out of here if you want." She holds her breath for his reply. Hair stands on the back of her neck.

"You wouldn't last long with me. I won't even last long. The dogs. They tell me I only get days where they have forever." He grabs fistfuls of his hair. "Stupid human brain!"

"What are you talking about? What dogs?" Sara tries to ignore the fear pulsating through her body.

"The ones that know you're here. They all know about you. The group of humans too afraid to leave their nest. But they'll come out. They always do." Carter stares at Sara with such intensity she involuntarily takes a step back.

"Carter, why is this happening? I… I love you." *Do I still love him?*

Carter slinks back into a darkened corner of his cell. "He knew. But he never loved you."

His words sting Sara. This isn't her Carter. She shouldn't care what he says right now. *He doesn't mean it.* She shakes her head and turns to leave.

"Watch Sydney." Carter's words slip through the darkness behind her. Anger fights some of the fear filling her. Sydney? He can care about Sydney but not her? *Oh, I'll watch her.*

Carter

Carter watches Tyler enter the room behind Sara. Even though he doesn't want Sara in the way she wants him, a primal urge heightens hatred in his chest for Tyler. *He wants her.*

Carter hurls himself at the bars. Their metal doesn't give under his strength. A growl rumbles through his chest as he tries again. His heart thunders in his chest. Harder. And harder. The pressure feels like it could break his sternum.

Tyler raises his gun. Sara watches in wide eyed horror. Carter pushes on the bars even harder, forcing his body past its limits. His heart pounds harder.

And then it stops.

But he doesn't.

His muscles no longer feel the pain of the strain he was putting on them. The metal doesn't hurt his hands as he beats on it. He can smell the fear soaking off the people in front of him. He needed them. Not to change them. Just to taste them.

One of the people pulls out a radio. The words don't matter. Carter knows more are coming. He revels in the thought of a feast.

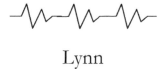

Lynn

In the small staff room, Lynn and Sydney prepare dinner consisting of the canned green beans and tuna collected from the police station. They scoop a small portion size of each onto the paper plates they've used for the past few days. They're lightly stained from yesterday's baked beans, but they only have so many. In black sharpie, their names stand out on the lip of each plate.

As Lynn reaches the eleventh plate with Olivia's name written in her bubbly handwriting, she cringes, dropping the metal spoon and causing a light clatter on the hardwood floor. *Why wasn't that thrown away days ago?*

Sydney looks at Lynn, then at the plate. Understanding softens her facial features and she puts her arm around Lynn's shoulders. "I know. I almost did the same thing."

Why can't we all survive? Lynn slowly bends down for the spoon, tossing it in the sink with the other dirty ones, and takes a few deep breaths. Her thoughts always circle back to her husband. *Is he alive? Am I finally free from him? How will I get to Lucas?* She has to keep telling herself that somehow Lucas is alive. *But if he isn't, well, it's better than being with Daniel.* As she calms down, a muffled gunshot sends her heart into another panic. In the familiar silence she's grown accustomed to in the past week, it might as well have been a bomb that went off.

Lynn looks at Sydney with wide eyes. "Where do you think that came from?"

Sydney shrugs unable to form words. Will pokes his head into the staff room. "Mason and I are going over to check on the gang at the police station. Maybe some of them got inside. They may be in trouble. Stay here and stay sharp."

The four that remain sit on their blanket beds and nibble at their food. Tyler and Sara had called for Officer Chase to join them at the police station but never said why. Now there's a gunshot, and Will and Mason are gone. It feels like hours pass but Lynn knows it's only been about twenty minutes. She doesn't hear anymore gunshots and can't decide if that's a good thing or a bad thing. She takes a sip from her water bottle. The room temperature liquid slips down her dry throat. *We're running out.* Everyone limits themselves to two bottles a day max, but between the cases they had stocked here and the couple from the police station, they might have enough for another two days, maybe three. No one has said anything, but she can't be the only one thinking it.

A few minutes later, there's a knock at the back door. Tyler and Sydney hop up to move the heavy kennels out of the way. Will walks in, followed by Mason, Officer Chase, Tyler, and Sara. All have sorrow-filled eyes. Lynn's heart drops. *Oh no.*

"Carter turned," Will says in a flat tone. "There was nothing Officer Chase could have done differently. He stopped him before he could hurt anyone."

"But I thought he was scratched? Most of us have been scratched. Does that mean we could all turn?" Sydney asks.

Will shakes his head. "I found a bite mark on his stomach. I think Carter was too afraid to tell us the truth. I understand the fear, but if any of you lie like that, it could put all of us in danger. If something like this happens again, let us know so we can handle it the best we can."

No one cries. Lynn thinks they were all expecting the worst since that's what's happened these past few days. *It's funny what you can get used to so quickly.* She swallows an extra antidepressant, and the nine of them eat in silence. Lynn and Sydney finish their turn on kitchen duty by gathering plates and sealing leftovers. They add Carter's portions back to the cans. *Waste not.*

Sydney

Sydney walks to the other end of the room, needing a moment to herself to not really think about anything. Josie paws her leg and meows softly. *How wonderful it must be to have no clue what's going on.* Sydney scoops her up into her arms, laying her on her back, and scratches under her chin. She migrates to Josie's kennel and tosses some food into her bowl. *At least you don't have to worry about where your next meal is coming from.*

Officer Chase approaches. Sydney doesn't blame him for killing Carter. What other choice did he have? Still, she can't bring herself to face him, so she continues to pet Josie hoping he'll go away.

No such luck. "How are you holding up, Sydney?" He asks, concern dipping into his tone.

"I'm fine."

"You know, that's usually code for a cry for help."

This time, Sydney turns to face the man. "Who here isn't crying for help?" She doesn't mean for her anger to come out on him, but she doesn't try to cover it up either. He nods, which only frustrates her more. *How can he be so calm?* She turns her back once again. "Is there something you need from me?"

"I wanted to apologize for the loss of your friend and give you this." He holds out his hand, which is holding Carter's smartwatch. The face is black since he hasn't been able to charge it, but he had still been wearing it with the plastic rainbow band out of habit. "I know you all have been keeping a personal item from your friends. It's a nice thought. I didn't know Carter until last week, so I didn't know what you'd want from him, but I thought this would be good enough." He glances down at his feet, appearing to feel awkward.

Sydney takes the watch. "Thanks."

Officer Chase continues to speak—even as Sydney wishes he would leave so she can grieve alone. "I truly am sorry. I was left here to protect everyone, and I keep failing."

Sydney's anger begins to dissipate. "It's not your fault. You're only one person and this is the zombie apocalypse."

"I should be better though. I should be a better leader. Do you know the last thing I said to Olivia? I told her if she didn't listen to me then she'd get herself killed."

Sydney's heart aches. *That's heavy.* There's nothing she can say to console him, so she takes his hand in hers and gives it a squeeze. That's what Carter would have done.

Officer Chase gives her hand an awkward squeeze back then walks away. At the pharmacy counter Sydney places the watch next to the other items. She brushes her fingers over the cool metal of the jewelry and keys. Olivia's hair scrunchie still has a few loose strands of her short black hair.

Later that evening, Sydney slides under her blankets. Carter's empty bed still lays beside her, so she stares up at the ceiling. Will emerges from the office with Erin and Officer Chase, and instead of going to bed, he clears his throat. Sydney sits up and looks at him in the limited light only provided by the moon.

"I know it's late guys, but I have some things to say. What happened today with Carter is hard on all of us. He wasn't just a coworker, he was a friend, and a great person. That goes the same for Olivia, Carla, Chris, Melissa, and Susan. I don't have words to describe the loss I feel, but we can't let this pull us apart. We need to watch out for each other more than ever."

"What's the point in surviving?" Sara's empty voice doesn't sound sleepy, just hollow.

Will rubs his chin. "We have been talking about some possibilities for the future, but for right now, I need you all to try and get some sleep tonight. Tomorrow we're headed to the tool rental store down the road where we should find a generator. We need electric so we have water, and this is our best chance."

The silence stretches on, and since Sydney can't see Will, she takes that as a sign he's finished talking. She wiggles back down in her bed and closes her eyes. The events of the day have exhausted her mind and body, and she falls asleep easier than she thought she would.

Day ten
Tyler

In the morning, Tyler wakes before the sun. He trudges into the staff room and sifts through his backpack. His deodorant stick wasn't full before the end of the world happened, and now it takes a couple twists for the gel to reach the surface. With no running water and the nearest creek at least a half mile into the woods, everyone tries to stay as fresh as they can with hand lotion and Febreze, but that luxury is running out as well. Maybe if the generator mission works, they will be able to shower.

One by one, everyone else crawls out of bed. Tyler

sits at the staff room table between Sara and Tiffany as Will points at a hand drawn map. "This is us." He points to a square with a squiggly line, representing the short driveway, connected to a long straight line. "This is Route 15. Here is Hardy's Tools." He points to another square. "If we follow the road, we can hit these three houses on the way and look for food, and maybe even find other survivors."

"How many of us are going?" Mason asks, already volunteering himself.

"Realistically I'd like to have five, "Officer Chase replies. "The generator will be heavy, and while Will and I can probably carry it most of the way, we'd do better trading out carriers. We also need people available to keep a look out and carry gas containers."

"Where will we get gas for the generator? Sheetz is miles away." Tiffany slumps on the table.

"We can syphon the gas from our cars," Officer Chase answers.

"But the zombies sabotaged our cars. All the gas is on the ground."

"Not all of it. If they broke the gas line on all the vehicles, then the gas in the line is what's on the ground. The rest stays in the tank unless the car is started. We're not going to make anyone go that doesn't want to. The risk is very high considering what happened to Olivia and Carter, but this is something we need to do to survive."

Erin clears her throat. "It's not just about survival. Will and I have been talking about what we can do to fight this. With the diagnostic equipment and my lab work background, we might be able to create a type of immunity."

"You're talking about finding a cure for the zombie apocalypse?" Tiffany arches an eyebrow skeptically.

"Not a cure, but maybe knowing more about these people when they turn will help us create a treatment for anyone recently bitten, at least to prolong the change until we can find them better help."

A spark of hope warms inside of Tyler.

Mason raises his hand. "I'll go." *Not surprising.*

"I went on the last suicide mission, and my leg is killing me from our last encounter. I'm sitting this one out." Tiffany exits the room.

Tyler and Lynn both agree to go while Erin says she will stay to protect the supplies. Sara stands to leave. "I don't much care about finding a cure. I'll just keep shooting until I can't anymore and that will be the end."

Sydney opts to stay behind as well since she isn't very gun savvy yet.

Will nods and everyone begins to empty the room. Tyler glances at Sara across the treatment area. Who is most in danger? The bigger group going out, or the small one staying in? One wrong move means everything. Tyler runs a finger over the scab on his arm from where the stick stabbed into it the other night. The accusatory thought that his blood caused the dogs to break in keeps replying in his mind. *No more mistakes.*

In the lobby, the other four making up the scavenging group wait. Officer Chase opens the front door and leads the group through the trap laid by the dogs.

Outside is the same empty quiet. There are no zombies in sight, other than the dead ones, so the group quickly reaches the main road. The first house comes up on the right. A little red car is parked out front with the same puddle of fluid. Officer Chase tries the door, and to Tyler's surprise, it opens. Everyone piles into the house. A dull groan comes from the living room and Will cautiously follows it. A zombie pops around the corner. Will pulls out a knife which was tucked into his boot and stabs at the creature's chest. The wounds don't seem to affect him as he keeps lunging. Will comes at it from the side, sliding the blade straight through its temple. It crumples to the ground, and Will retrieves his knife.

The rest of the house is empty as they search for food. A kid's school bag from upstairs proves useful for loading up the cans. Tyler finds a crowbar on the front porch and trades his broom stick handle for it. Back out on the street, Officer Chase instructs Lynn to leave the bag for the return trip. "No use wasting the energy carrying it there and carrying it back."

The next two houses are uneventful, providing a few more bags of food and some toiletries, which they leave in the middle of the road for easy pick up. Hardy's square pale-yellow building comes into view along with three dogs. The five scavengers retrieve their weapons, hoping for a silent victory. Officer Chase swings his baton at the first dog. Mason hurls himself at a smaller dog about to lunge at Lynn.

In front of Tyler stands a large German Shepherd, blood dripping from the fur around its mouth. Its teeth are bared as he stalks closer. Tyler's hand tightens on the crowbar. *I'm really going to do this?* The dog throws himself at Tyler who swings his weapon at the dog's head. The sickening crack of its skull echoes in Tyler's head. The dog falls to the ground.

Bile rises up Tyler's throat and he's unable to keep his breakfast down. Vomit climbs up his esophagus and spews out his mouth until there's nothing left in his stomach. His head spins making him feel even more nauseous. He just killed a dog when his whole career was meant to save them. He quickly collects himself and continues to follow the group to the rental building.

Will tries the door, but this time, it's locked. Seeing no other option, he smashes the butt of his gun into the glass and reaches through the hole to unlock the door. Inside the dusty tool rental building, it's dark. Officer Chase pulls out his flashlight and shines it over the shelves full of drills and small circular saws. A wall to Tyler's left is full of hanging weed eaters and leaf blowers. In the middle of the floor is a massive zero turn mower.

The group creeps through the dark toward the back. Two large generators occupy the corner near the checkout counter. Tyler grabs a few empty orange gas containers. Will and Officer Chase ready themselves to lift the machine when a voice breaks the silence.

"What do you think you all are doing?"

A man stands behind the counter, holding a shotgun aimed at Tyler.

Chapter Nine

Day ten
Tiffany

Tiffany crouches over her bag in the staff room. She sifts through the extra change of clothes all vet techs learn to carry, though they were dirtied days ago, just like the ones she's wearing. *God, we stink!* Her bottle of Hydrocodone rattles lightly, and she looks around, making sure no one heard it. She could get another bottle; she has the chance. She hasn't taken any of the pills herself yet, but maybe she should start. This whole situation would seem a little less fucked up if she did. It would also dull the constant throbbing in her leg.

Some days are harder than others when saying no to returning to that lifestyle. Tiffany remembers every second of the high she lived on. Between the lustful sex with Brent and the drugs, she loved the oblivious state that allowed her to pass through life without a problem or a care. Until she was caught and sent to rehab. The withdrawal period was agony, and there were days she wished she could die and get it over with. But once she was released, the new life before her seemed limitless. She went to college and pursued a veterinary technician career. It wasn't long until her old friends found out though, and she had Brent blowing up her phone for a fix.

Loud voices carry themselves to her as Erin and Sara argue. "I don't know why you won't just let me go!" Sara shouts. "You aren't in control of me!"

"I'm trying to keep you safe!" Erin retorts. "You saw how those things attack. They will swarm you. You're acting selfish by risking all of our safety."

There's silence, then moments later, Sara enters the staff room. Tiffany jolts at the sound of her footsteps and quickly tries to bury her stash. "Uh, I'm just looking for some Tylenol," she offers in defense, but Sara seems uninterested.

"I don't care what you're doing." She slumps on the couch, hands gripping her pistol.

Tiffany's brow scrunches and she goes to join her friend. "What was all the yelling about?" She thinks of putting her arm around Sara, but due to the way she's changed the past few days, she doesn't make the move. The girl beside her is so different from her friend. Sara has always been so full of life and love. Tiffany thinks back on all the nights they would stay up late gossiping over margaritas. Even when Sara found out she was pregnant; her determination outshined her fear of choosing to raise her daughter alone.

"I want to kill them."

"Kill who?" Tiffany's heart pounds.

Sara whips her head around to glare at Tiffany. The coldness in her eyes is so unfamiliar. "The zombies, or whatever the hell they are! They ruined my life! They killed my friends, my daughter, and Carter. They're worthless creatures that deserve their heads blown off."

"I agree with you Sara, but you can't do it all on your own. There's too many." This time Tiffany does allow her hand to reach for Sara's arm.

Sara jerks away and stands up. "I don't see anyone else trying. Everyone wants to find a cure and help these monsters and you're sitting in here counting your pills."

Tiffany's mouth goes dry. Any reply she had to calm her friend down gets lost in the deafening pounding in her ears.

$$\sim\!\!\bigwedge\!\!\!-\!\!\bigwedge\!\!\!-\!\!\bigwedge\!\!\!\sim$$

Lynn

Lynn stares at the threat in front of her. The burly man with the gun has a full grey beard and a tattered flannel shirt. Tuffs of white hair stick out from under his green ball cap with the store's logo printed on the front. The rifle in his large hands bounces back and forth from Tyler to Will.

Finally, Officer Chase finds his voice. He holds his hands up in a surrender position and steps closer to the counter. "Sir, we mean you no trouble. We're half of a larger group up at the vet clinic. We're trying to get power so we have water to survive. If you're not infected, you can come with us. We have food and protection."

The man mulls over the officer's words. "I'd appreciate some food. I don't know the last time I ate." The man stands and walks around the counter toward the cop and extends his hand. "I'm Jim. I used to work here, guess maybe I'm unemployed now."

Officer Chase shakes Jim's hand. I'm Chase. This is Dr. Will, Tyler, Mason, and Lynn." He gestures to each of them in turn. "There's four others back at the hospital. You haven't been bitten, have you?"

"No sir. You're the first to come in here and so far, none of you have bit me." He winks in Lynn's direction. She inwardly shutters. Why does he remind her of her husband so much?

Maybe it was the wink. Daniel would always wink at her in public after making an inappropriate comment or joke. She would always blush, wondering what other people thought of his openness. He was never flirty at home, though. What he wanted, he got, it didn't matter if she wasn't in the mood, or if she was busy, or even if Lucas was just in the next room watching TV. Lynn shoves the thought away. *Daniel isn't here.*

With the tension easing, Officer Chase and Will begin to lift the generator. Their grunts of effort ensure a swap of carriers will need to happen sooner than they planned. Lynn grabs a gas container and holds one door open while Mason holds the other. She gives him a bashful smile. *Stop thinking about Daniel. I can think about Mason now.*

The sun is blinding initially, but Lynn welcomes it. She hated being confined in darkness. Hopefully, the generator will make the hospital feel a little homier. She reveled in the idea of a shower and a hot meal. But the generator offered a different glimmer of hope to everyone else. A hope for a cure. Did she want a cure? Not really. Not that she wanted anyone else to die, but a cure meant possibly returning everything to normal and going home, and she never wanted to return to Daniel. Somehow, she would have to save Lucas from him though.

The first of the three houses they raided comes into view. Once they reach it, Lynn grabs one of the bags they left and hoists it on her shoulder. Will and Officer Chase set the generator down for a break. Mason and Jim offer to take a turn, but Will assures them they're good for now.

The group continues again, making a stop at the second and third house, picking up supplies and resituating the generator. Lynn can make out the driveway to the clinic. *Almost home.*

The chilling harmony of growls and snarls causes everyone to stop their slow progress toward safety. Lynn turns and finds a pack of at least a dozen dogs staring at them. The various breeds circle their small group.

Will and Officer Chase set the generator down and pull out their guns. A quiet fight won't work this time. Lynn sets her four packs down and grabs her gun, aiming it at a black lab closest to her.

The moment stretches on as each side waits for the other to attack first. Lynn takes a hesitant step back, trying to near the rest of the group. Her foot snaps a twig and the time-locked moment breaks as the dogs lunge forward in unison. The lab barrels into her. She swings an elbow to knock it away then aims her gun before it can pounce again. The sound of her gunshot is lost in the roar of the others as each person fights to defend themselves.

Lynn shoots two more and begins to think the group will escape, but when she looks in the direction of the hospital, her heart sinks. Another pack of dogs, accompanied by a few humans, move quickly in their direction. "Incoming!" she shouts as the others dispatch the last of the first attackers. She watches as their bodies stiffen with the sight of the new oncoming threat.

Her heart drums hard as adrenaline pumps through her veins. The second wave reaches them before they have time to shoot any. Mason swings his gun around skillfully, taking down the three dogs encircling Lynn. She nods at him in thanks. *I owe him more than a nod.* She allows a small smile to creep across her face before a yell pulls her back to reality.

"We need to move before another group comes!" Will shouts. He lifts the generator with Officer Chase for the final time, and they all move as swiftly as they can. The driveway is only a few yards away.

A third wave peaks over the hill from the direction of the police station. Will and Officer Chase quicken their steps up the driveway. Mason, Tyler, and Lynn walk backwards with their guns aimed at the threat. *We're not going to make it.* Lynn fires off the first shot, taking down a Jack Russel. The group continues to shoot as the men continue carrying the generator, determined not to stop this time.

Tyler takes down several dogs, but then the zombies reach the group. Mason holds his gun but doesn't shoot. A short woman with scraggly grey hair and ripped clothes leaps at him, knocking his gun away. He lands on his back and holds her shoulders. White fur sticks out of her mouth, and her teeth snap inches away from Mason's face. Lynn watches, frozen in place. She's forced herself not to look at the zombies for fear of recognizing one, but this woman pulls at her memories. "Mrs. Croft?" The former client shows no reaction to hearing her name. *What do I do?* Lynn knows Mason won't hurt a person, living or dead. He's said it before. Mason fights to throw her off but her inhuman strength makes it a harder task.

Lynn snaps out of her trance and rushes to Mason. His attacker quits trying to bite and now rips at his shirt. Her fingers work like claws as the fabric shreds away, and his bare chest lays vulnerable. With little trouble, the woman shreds through his skin just as she had his shirt. Mason's screams alert everyone else, and they recoil as his insides become visible.

Lynn brings the butt of her gun down on the zombie wiggling atop her friend. It doesn't faze her much, it does stop her movements long enough for Lynn to put a bullet between her eyes. Mason lays on the ground, gasping. The gashes through his midsection are deep. Lynn forces him to sit up and continues to remove his shirt. He groans in agony to protest, but she ignores him. She wads his shirt and presses it tight against his abdomen. They're too close to home to give up now.

Tyler and Jim look around for more attackers, but nothing comes. Lynn helps Mason to his feet and supports him as he takes shaky steps. "Come on. We'll get you patched up soon. We're almost there."

Mason gurgles a response as he hangs onto

consciousness.

Officer Chase's scream snaps her attention away. A zombie stands behind him, sinking its teeth into his neck. Blood squirts from an artery and as the zombie tears a chunk of flesh off with its teeth. The officer drops his end of the generator before Will can let go of his. The heavy machine crashes down on Will's right hand and he lets out a yell of his own. Tyler and Jim rush over to maneuver the generator off his hand. They pick it up and begin the last leg of the journey, slower than the other men had moved. With his left hand, Will puts a bullet into the head of the zombie still tearing into Officer Chase.

Lynn can see the door to the clinic. She supports even more of Mason's weight as he starts to slump into her. *I won't let him die.*

Sydney

All the gunshots outside put Sydney on edge. Part of her wants to go to her friends, but she knows she wouldn't be much help.

Each round of bullets raises both her fear and her pain. She can feel the dogs dying. Every one of them. Sara and Tiffany keep asking to go out and fight with their friends, but Erin keeps discouraging them, saying they have to stay together. Sydney paces the room, muttering to herself. "There's too many." Then there's banging on the broken glass on the back door.

Erin and Tiffany rush to it and pull back the kennels. Lynn pushes through, supporting most of

Mason's weight. His eyes droop and he clutches a blood-soaked shirt against his bare stomach. Sydney's heart pounds. Tyler—and another man she doesn't recognize—carry a generator through the door. Will comes in last, backing through with his gun still raised, but in his left hand. His right hand is tucked tightly against his chest. He lowers his gun and begins to move the kennels.

"Where's Officer Chase?" Erin asks, fearing the answer.

"Probably out there with the hoard by now." Will directs Tyler and the man to the back storage room where a side exit door leads to the hook up for a generator. Tiffany takes them one of the gas containers. Lynn lays Mason on the ground and talks to him in a hushed tone.

"What happened out there? Who is that other man?" Erin reaches for Will's apparent injured hand, but he brushes her away.

"His name is Jim. The rest isn't important right now. We need to get Mason into surgery." He motions for Lynn, Sydney, and Erin to carry him into the surgery room. They lay him on the table. He's long since passed out from blood loss.

The loud hum of the generator breaks the silence and the lights throughout the building illuminate their faces. "Will, if he was bit, you know he can't stay here."

"He wasn't bit. They tore him open with their hands."

"But your hand is injured. How will you be able to operate?" Erin shifts uncomfortably on her feet.

Will steadies his gaze at her. "You'll need to do it."

Erin stiffens. "You know I can't—"

Will cuts her off. "Don't give me that. I know you can. This won't be any different than a dog, and you were taught surgery the same as I was. You can do this."

"That's been years ago. And I haven't had much practice since."

"We don't have another choice." The weight of his words seems to sit heavy on Erin.

Erin takes a deep breath. "Okay, Lynn and Tyler, work on getting a catheter in Mason. We will also need blood for a transfusion. Is anyone here O negative?"

Tiffany runs off to get a surgical pack and several sterile laparotomy pads. She returns with Sara in tow. "O negative."

"Great. If you draw her blood into a blood bag, we can get started immediately." Erin's voice is even, but Sydney can hear the nervousness underneath.

"I'm not saving a monster." Sara turns to walk away, but Will grabs her arm.

"He wasn't bit. He's not infected. You would be saving Mason."

"You don't know he's not infected. You don't know anything about these things." She shrugs Will off and leaves the group.

Sydney lets out a sigh. "I'm O negative, just don't like needles."

Tiffany's eyes light up. "Neither do the animals that come in here. Challenge accepted." She leaves to grab the supplies. Erin nods and begins scrubbing her hands. In surgery, Lynn and Tyler have Mason hooked up to anesthesia, fluids, and a monitor. A surgical pack is near the table. Erin's gloved hands set to opening it.

"It's okay Erin. I'm going to be right here with

you." Will's soft voice carries out to Sydney. *He whispered that. And I heard it.*

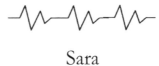

Sara

Sara taps her fingers against her gun in the staff room. With everyone preoccupied with Mason's surgery, she feels completely alone. Which was fine by her. She didn't see any point in wasting the gas or energy on reviving a monster. All she wanted to do was kill them.

Sydney raps her knuckles on the door frame, startling Sara. "Hey."

Sara only spares her a glance. *She can't even shoot the monsters. She won't last long.* "Hi," she mumbles.

"They were wanting a few of us who aren't helping with the surgery to go syphon some gas. They took as much blood from me as they could, but I still want to be useful. Would you want to help me? The dogs have wondered off."

Sara rolls her eyes but stands. A shower sounds so good, and they'll need more gas since they're using it all for the pointless surgery. Plus, Carter told her to watch Sydney. Maybe she can find out why.

The two techs walk out into the parking lot, careful to look all around them. Bodies litter the parking lot. Each have two empty gas containers. When they reach the first car, Sydney reveals one of the tubes used for suction in surgery and a large 60mL syringe. Sara raises an eyebrow. She's never syphoned gas, so part of her is curious how it will work.

Sydney tapes the syringe to one end of the tubing,

making sure it's attached securely and airtight. She opens the gas tank on the first car and the lid on the gas container. Once the open end of the tubing is lowered into the gas tank, she pulls back on the plunger of the syringe until it pops out. She drops the syringe end of the tubing into the gas container, and just moments pass before Sara hears the sound of the flowing liquid.

"How do you know how to do this?"

"My dad taught me because he never had money for gas." Sydney blushes.

"So, he had you steal for him?" Sara's jaw drops in shock.

Sydney's face becomes even more red. "Yeah, since I was smaller, I was less noticeable. I came up with the syringe part on my own though. He taught me to suck on the hose with my mouth to get it to start but sometimes it would end up in my mouth, and it tasted awful." Her nose crinkles in disgust.

Sara averts her gaze back to the stream of gas. Sydney had talked about her past before, but it's something she's usually kept pretty private.

After they fill their containers, the two girls head back toward the clinic. Two zombies come around the corner of the building. Sara pulls out her gun and aims it at the first one, but Sydney puts her hand on the barrel to lower it.

"Wait," Sydney whispers. "There's more close by. If we're quiet, we can sneak past them. The humans don't see well."

"How the hell do you know that?" Sara asks skeptically.

Sydney stiffens. "I've just watched them and that's

what I've seen. Trust me, okay?"

Sara gives a quick nod but watches Sydney closely. They crouch and inch across the gravel. When the zombies look their way, the girls freeze. The retreat back to safety is slow, but Sydney knew what she was talking about.

Once inside, Sara rises from her crouch. Sydney takes the gas to the back room. *I understand now.*

Erin and Will are still in surgery with Mason, their muffled voices audible as Will talks Erin through things she's unsure about. The relationship is beautiful to an outsider, but Sara doesn't feel anything when looking at them. Could she have had that with Carter?

Thinking about her losses gets her blood pumping again. Anger rises inside her, and she thinks about going to unplug the generator to halt the surgery. The idea excites her as she thinks of it as killing another one of the monsters. Mason is dead to her anyways. She'd be doing him a favor by stopping the progression of the infection.

But she only thinks about the idea.

Chapter Ten

Day ten
Tyler

Tyler notices Erin glance at the clock on the wall for the hundredth time since being in the surgery room. His legs ache from standing still for hours, and his rumbling stomach makes his head feel a little woozy. With Will's guidance, Erin has successfully stopped several bleeders in Mason's abdomen. The fluids and fresh blood being pumped into Mason's veins has helped keep his vitals steady throughout the procedure. Each time Erin stops another bleeder they return to more normal levels.

The distressed cry of the monitor causes all three to look at the machine as Mason's vitals begin to plummet.

Erin maneuvers everything in Mason's abdominal

cavity looking for the cause. The longer she looks, the more her hands begin to tremble.

"Calm down, you can do this," Will says reassuringly.

Erin's face alights red. "You keep telling me that, but I keep telling you I can't!"

Tyler's own panic rises as the monitor blares. What can he do? How can he help? A thought comes to him. "Do you know why I tell jokes at inappropriate times?"

"Not now, Tyler," Will dismisses, but Tyler continues anyway.

"I do it because I hate feeling uncomfortable. I don't know what else to say in the quiet. I don't know how to tell the girl I love she's so important to me. I don't know how to comfort my friends over Olivia's death, or Carter's. So, I shut my brain off and babble, and usually a joke comes out because I'm secretly hoping it will be what someone needs."

Erin's now looking at her tech.

"So, turn your brain off Erin. Stop feeling scared and unsure and just tell me what comes to your mind. Let your hands do the work they know how to do."

Erin stays quiet for several seconds then takes a deep breath. "I know I shouldn't be this unnerved to do surgery, but I wasn't lying when I said I was out of practice. Every surgery done at the hospital for the past ten years has either been by Will or Heather. All of them but one." Erin's hands begin moving inside Mason again. Slower this time.

"Will was away at a conference and Heather was out of town with family," she adds. "The day had been relatively quiet, and any emergency needing surgery I sent to an ER hospital in the city. In the late afternoon,

Mason came into the treatment area carrying a bloated dog with what looked like a twisted stomach. The owners begged me to save him, and there wasn't time for them to transport him somewhere else, so I had to try, right?" The monitor returns to a steadier rhythm.

"I remember all the blood. The lights feeling too bright. My heart racing as I pulled from my classes for what I should do. After two hours in surgery, I could tell the procedure was hopeless. The dog had passed, and even though Will assured me I probably did everything right and that it was just a poor prognosis, the event still leaves me unsure of myself. I hope the outcome will be different this time."

With a gloved hand, Will reaches into Mason's body maneuvering what he needs to in order to look for any more bleeders. "I think you got them all."

Tyler doesn't dare relax yet. Even though that would mean the hard part is over, luck hasn't been on their side lately. Erin completes her own double check and begins removing laparotomy pads. As she sows the wound shut, the tenseness in her shoulders eases.

All her techs huddle outside the surgery door window, waiting for the news of a success. All of them except Sara. Tyler wonders where she is, but more importantly, what's happened to her. This situation is starting to change them in small ways, but Sara is like a whole other person.

With the last staples in place in Mason's skin, Erin takes a step back with a look of disbelief. She did it. She saved him. Her breath catches, and Will wraps his arms around her, pulling her in. A few tears of relief fall down her cheeks before she exits the room. Tyler watches her through the window in the door as she smiles at the worried faces pleading for answers. "Mason's surgery went well." Tyler's relief spreads across the techs' faces. "He will need rest, and probably more blood if we can get it, but he should be okay. We can take turns keeping a watchful eye on him."

Outside, the sun has long since set, but the fluorescent lights create a more familiar and comfortable atmosphere. Erin's body slumps with exhaustion. Lynn offers to take the first watch over Mason, and Erin agrees only after making her promise to wake her immediately if anything changes.

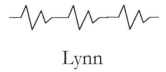

Lynn

Lynn slouches against the wall and holds Mason's hand. The hours drag by slowly, but she doesn't mind. Mason's even breathing gives her comfort. She didn't care he wouldn't shoot Mrs. Croft to save himself. To her, that made him even more incredible. She only wished she could have saved him herself. Why had she hesitated when he was attacked? It had only been a few seconds, but it had made all the difference. *Obviously.*

A small clatter from the staff room makes Lynn jump. Her heart hammers in her chest. Could zombies get in through the small window in the staff room? Wouldn't she have heard glass? Yes, she would. So, if not zombies, what was it? Someone taking advantage of indoor plumbing? But she hadn't seen anyone get up. They must have been very sneaky.

Her legs itch to investigate. She checks Mason's breathing and heart rate one more time before clambering to her feet. She creeps through the darkness toward the staff room and hovers in the doorway, trying to see who is up this late.

Jim is on the floor, bent over a bag with his back to Lynn. He appears to be filling it with something, but it's too dark for Lynn to tell what it is. She takes a deep breath and clears her throat.

Jim startles and turns to look at her. "Oh, uh, Lindsey, right?"

"Lynn."

"Right, Lynn. What are you doing up?" Jim stands, kicking the bag out of sight.

"I've been up watching over my friend. What are you doing?" Her eyes linger to the bag halfway hidden beside the end of the couch.

"Couldn't sleep. I guess I got used to being on my own and not having the chance to. Maybe if I had a pretty woman like you to sleep next to, things would be different."

Hair raises on the back of Lynn's neck at his suggestion. Her stomach turns because her thoughts involuntarily circle back to her husband. Without replying or investigating further, she leaves the staff room and returns to Mason's side.

Day thirteen
Sydney

Anticipation bubbles in Sydney as the new day begins. Yesterday was spent logging the food and other supplies gathered from the houses and cycling everyone through a long overdue shower. The cold water came as a shock on her skin and made her shiver at first, but a shower had never felt so refreshing. The scavenging team had even brought an assortment of shampoos and soaps back with them. It was the biggest luxury available in the past two weeks.

Today, however, was even better in her mind. Today, Will and Erin plan on working on running diagnostics on the infected to see what they can learn. Sydney knows she doesn't have advanced lab skills, but she is more than ready to help in any way she can.

Will already switched over the generator to just the lab equipment since they require more power. Erin glances through some of the manuals, refreshing herself on tests she hadn't ran in a while. Tiffany gears herself up for the important part.

Capturing a zombie.

Will wants to see a CT scan of the infected brain and Erin wants to run a few blood tests. The tranquilizer gun won't work since their blood isn't circulating, and bullets don't faze them unless they're in the head, and that wouldn't help.

No, they'll have to bait one.

With live bait.

The only two realistic things they have for live bait are Jake or Josie, neither of which lessens the dread in the pit of Sydney's stomach. Will assures her they will be smart and quick about it and hopefully no harm will come to the animal. But things happen.

Since Josie can fit in a cat carrier, Will comes up with a plan. He draws a bit of her blood up into a syringe then shoves her in the carrier. Outside the back door he places the carrier a few yards away then squirts her blood on the ground around her.

Sydney and the other techs sit in the vet truck and Will's personal truck armed with guns in case this goes wrong. Will stands inside the back door with a catch pole in hand. Sydney watches Josie's paw dip in and out of the cage, looking for freedom. Her heart pounds in her chest. Whispers flood Sydney's mind. Her brow furrows in concentration as she tries to make out the words. A chant saying "blood" over and over grows clearer by the second. *What is happening to me?*

Two huskies and four zombies appear from around the corner of the building. They reach the carrier in only seconds. Sydney can't see what they're doing. *Did they get Josie?* Tiffany opens the truck door and lands a shot on one of the zombies. The body crumples to the ground. The others don't seem to be phased as the smell of fresh blood consumes their attention. Will exits the building and loops the end of the pole around one of the husky's heads. The dog snarls and pulls against the restraint, fighting to get free, but Will pulls him inside.

Erin takes the pole from Will and hands him another. Sydney opens her door and aims at a zombie who is now holding the carrier. She fires but misses. A second shot hits the zombie in the shoulder. The force of the impact causes him to drop the carrier, but he goes right back for it. Sydney fires again at the same time Tiffany does. The zombie drops. *Which one of us got him?*

Will holds his second pole up high and loops it around one of the remaining zombies. The larger body proves harder to hold. Jim emerges from one of the trucks and helps the doctor drag the flailing prisoner inside the hospital.

The techs finish off the remaining attackers then rush inside. Sydney makes a quick stop for Josie's carrier then follows the rest. Inside she holds the carrier up, peering inside. Josie cowers against the back, ears pinned against her head. Sydney sets the carrier down on one of the treatment tables and goes to open the door.

Sara pulls Sydney's hand away. "What do you think you're doing?"

"I'm going to let Josie out. She's terrified."

"She could be infected. She needs to be shot."

Sydney flinches at how casually Sara mentions the death of their beloved office pet. "The carrier wasn't broken, so she wasn't bit."

"I don't care!" Her voice rises and sounds strange coming from her small body. "We don't need to take any chances. What if it works differently than we think?"

"You're not killing her!" Sydney doesn't have control over her emotions. There's only a primal urge to protect. She pushes Sara away from the carrier and goes for the latch again.

Sara barely stumbles and launches herself at Sydney, knocking her off her feet. She lands on top of Sydney, whose back hits the hard floor. They tussle against each other until stronger arms pull them apart. Tyler encircles his arms around Sara while Will holds back Sydney's hands. The two women glare at each other.

Will eases his grip on Sydney and reaches for Josie's carrier. "Sara is right, we don't know how this works, so we shouldn't release Josie immediately." He holds up a hand to silence Sydney's protests. "But Sydney is also right, we shouldn't kill her without a reason. We can put her in her cage and see if she begins acting different."

Tyler eases his grip on Sara.

She shrugs off his hands resting lightly on her upper arms. "You all are idiots." She storms off toward the staff room.

Sara

Once in the staff room, Sara paces back and forth, muttering to herself. "I'm trying to keep everyone safe while everyone just wants to play house." She stops her ranting once she remembers Mason was moved to the couch in the staff room to rest more comfortably while recovering.

Sara turns to stare at him. His chest is bare, and the line of staples up his abdomen remind her of the stupid surgery he went through. He should be dead. She envisions him turning and creeping through the dark quiet hospital during the night, ripping out the throats of her remaining friends. Their blood running like a river across the pale green floor.

She can't help herself. The impulse controls her muscles and she reaches for the gun tucked in the waistband of her newly cleaned pants. *I will be my own fucking hero*. She aims it at Mason's head, and without any remorse, she pulls the trigger.

Chapter Eleven

Day thirteen
Sydney

Everyone's running. *Why was there a gunshot?* Sydney's heart pounds, fearing zombies and dogs, but nothing prepares her for the truth.

In the staff room, Sara stares at Mason where he rests on the couch.

Except now there's a bullet hole in his forehead.

"What the fuck, Sara?" Tiffany exclaims when she gets into the room.

Erin stares with her hand over her mouth and Lynn stomps her way in front of Sara. "What is wrong with you? Why the hell did you kill Mason?" Her hands ball into fists at her side.

Will steps between the two girls and snatches Sara's gun from her hand. "That was out of line. What were you thinking?"

The annoyed expression on Sara's face doesn't faulter. "I am trying to keep us all safe! I don't get what's wrong with you all!"

"Erin spent hours doing that surgery for Mason and you ruined it." Sydney's own anger rises.

"I stopped him from turning and saved the group. Do I need to do the same with you?" Sara's glare challenges Sydney.

"Sara! That's enough." Erin finds her voice.

"No. Sydney needs to prove to me she hasn't been bitten. Right now."

"Why do you think *I've* been bitten?" Sydney gives the group a worried look. She didn't want to be locked up, left alone with the strange voices in her head.

"Carter told me to watch you, and you've been acting weird. Prove me wrong."

Erin takes Sydney's arm and walks her toward the employee bathroom. She grabs Sara on the way and the three enter the small room. She shuts the door and turns on the light. "Take your clothes off, Sydney," she says in an overly calm voice.

"You can't be serious?" Sydney asks exasperated.

"If this will satisfy Sara, then yes. But if she's clean, Sara, you'll drop this, understand?"

The girls nod, and Sydney begins to slide out of her clothes. Her face flushes with embarrassment as she strips completely down. Once naked, she does several turns, lifting her arms and turning her head until Erin allows her to get dressed.

They didn't find any bite marks.

When they exit, Will clears his throat. "Sara doesn't get a gun until I say so."

Sara stomps away without a word, and the rest of the group disperses except for Lynn who sobs over Mason a little longer.

Sydney shuts her eyes and wishes all this would end. Then her hair begins to stand on end. Something's happening. Someone's here.

A pounding on the backdoor doesn't startle her. That doesn't sound like the normal infected. She walks toward the door along with everyone else. Will reaches it first, peers around the kennels, and turns to look at Erin with wide eyes before pulling the metal barricade away.

Heather limps through the door. Her checkered shirt is torn at the shoulder and bloody splotches paint the blue and white fabric. Her dull eyes stare at us as she shuffles through the door.

Will raises his pistol. "Stop, Heather."

Her unfocused eyes look all around the room as if trying to discern where the sound came from.

Will raises his voice louder. "Heather, I said stop!"

Her attention snaps to him. "Help me." She collapses on the floor.

Day fourteen
Lynn

Lynn spins another tube of blood in the centrifuge. They are nowhere closer to finding answers than they were when Heather stumbled through the door. Once conscious, Will learned Colton was infected when he took her away. His behavior changed over the next few days until he finally snapped and bit her. She said she could feel the change happening and started working her way back to the hospital. She was attacked a few times in the beginning, but eventually the dogs and the humans started leaving her alone. She said she knew she was coming to the end. Heather says it takes about a week for humans to lose their minds.

And she's on day six.

She's locked in isolation now. Will wanted to take her to the police station like Carter, but Erin insisted she would be fine here. Without Officer Chase to make decisions, things feel less strict. Lynn tries to push the fear from her mind. Heather isn't a monster yet, but it's coming. Will keeps a close eye on Sara, knowing what she must be thinking.

Part of Lynn understands Sara's behavior, but a bigger part of her hates her for killing Mason. He was innocent. Lynn knew that much. It's a good thing her daughter isn't here, because no one should have a mother with a heart like that.

"Lynn, can you run a 4Dx on the infected blood?" Erin calls from her desk in the office.

"Do you think they have Lyme disease or something?" Lynn's eyebrows scrunch together at the odd request. 4Dx tests check for heartworms and tick-borne diseases like Lyme, anaplasmosis, and ehrlichia, none of which explains the behavior of the monsters outside.

"I'm just trying to cover all the bases."

Lynn sighs but pulls a Snap test from the box beside the centrifuge. She adds four drops of conjugate and three of the dog's blood sample to a tube to mix. She pours the mixture onto the test then snaps the activator when it's ready.

She didn't want to help with the researching, but when Erin asked, she agreed, hoping it would occupy her mind. She took the last of her antidepressants yesterday when she lost Mason. *I need to quit thinking about him. Focus on the blood tests.* But looking for a cause of the outbreak will lead to finding a cure, and finding a cure leads to her going back to Daniel. The zombies are tearing apart the world she knew, and she is okay with that. Scavenging and surviving isn't as bad as living with him.

But finding a cure could save Heather. That made the guilt inside Lynn raise to a head. *Does everyone have to die so I can be free?*

So far, their research efforts have proven fruitless. The CT of the dog and the human both showed severe brain swelling, which explains the aggression, but the rest of their bodies appear normal. The blood results show low red blood cells, hematocrit, and hemoglobin, but that could be dozens of diseases.

Halfway through the ten-minute test, Lynn starts to wonder if this is a tick-borne disease. Lyme disease can come with neurological symptoms. Is it possible this is an advanced mutated form? With the speed of the outbreak that would mean a lot of ticks very quickly.

Not ticks.

Mosquitos.

Lynn rushes over to the tech desk where several small baggies lay, each one with one of the weird new mosquitos. Before the outbreak, Will and Erin wanted to send some of the mosquitos they found to a lab for study purposes, so the techs had been bagging them up. "Erin, I think I'm on to something." Lynn grabs up the baggies and runs into the office.

Erin swivels around in her chair and looks up from one of the scientific journals she had been reading. "What is it?" She eyes the bags in Lynn's hands.

"These mosquitos just showed up. What if they're carrying the disease?"

Erin thinks for a moment. "That's very possible. And it would explain how it spread so quickly in the beginning." She pops out of her seat and takes one of the baggies from Lynn. "Let's dissect one and look at it under the microscope." She pulls a microscope slide from the drawer and using forceps and a scalpel blade she opens the mosquito's body.

While she prepares her sample, Lynn checks her 4Dx test. Not to her surprise, it's negative. A low groan from Erin pulls Lynn over to the microscope. "Have you found anything?"

"There's something here that looks suspicious, but it's small. Too small for me to tell what it is." Erin pulls away and walks off to find Will.

Will returns and looks through the microscope. He glides the slide around on the microscope table slowly as he scans for answers. When he pulls away, he has a similar look on his face as Erin did. "You're right. There is something there. Maybe a virus because of the size, but I'm not a hundred percent sure on that."

Will leaves to check on Heather. Erin twists a strand of her hair while deep in thought. "Can you prepare a blood smear for me?" She asks Lynn as she reaches for one of the nearby veterinary medicine books.

Lynn does what she is told. She carefully places a drop of blood on a slide and smears it with the edge of another. She dips the smeared slide into three different containers of stain then rinses the slide with water. She dries the back of the slide then sets it on the microscope for Erin.

Erin scans the slide on low power, then slowly, one by one, she moves up to a higher power. As she scans, Lynn's mind wanders.

If these mosquitos really are carrying a disease, a virus, where did they come from?

"I've got something." Erin's voice makes Lynn feel uneasy.

"What is it?" Despite her fear, Lynn wants to know.

"The monocytes and lymphocytes have inclusions. Granted, that could be a couple things, but I've seen something like this before."

"What does the inclusions mean?" Lynn looks over the page in the book Erin was browsing.

"Canine distemper."

"Those things outside don't look like any canine distemper-infected dogs I've ever seen."

"It's definitely an advanced case, but I'm almost certain."

Will returns from the staff room. "But Canine distemper isn't zoonotic. People wouldn't be infected."

Erin purses her lips, evidently not ready to give up on the small lead she's got. "What if it was mixed with something that is zoonotic. Something like Rabies?"

Lynn's jaw drops. How could those two just mix?

Will echoes her burning questions. "How could a mosquito just get lucky enough to carry a mutated form of two diseases?"

"I have a hunch. Let me go look through some of our latest vet medicine magazines. I think I know what's going on. In the meantime, give Heather any meds that could help."

Tyler

A scream startles Tyler from preparing everyone's dinner of hotdogs and green beans. He follows the running staff to the kennels on the far end of the treatment area. Sydney kneels on the floor, something white and fluffy clutched in her hands.

Josie.

As he looks closer, he can see blood smeared on the kennel and up one of Sydney's arms. Lots of blood.

Will pushes through into the room "What happened? Did she bite you?"

Through heavy sobs Sydney shakes her head and forces her voice out. "She was killed. I got here and her throat was slit."

A sick feeling enters Tyler's stomach. His eyes mimic those around him as they glance at Sara hanging at the back of the crowd. She doesn't back down from the stares but instead shrugs. "I stopped her before she turned."

Sydney leaps to her feet and spins around to face Sara. More blood soaks the front of her pink scrub top. "She wasn't going to turn!" She pushes her way through the people blocking her from pouncing on Sara, but Will grabs her arm and holds her back.

Tyler shifts his body in front of Sara's. Why does she have to keep doing stupid things? He can't keep protecting her. Tiffany looks like she wants to yell, and Sydney could tear her limb from limb if he let her. Part of him wants to step aside…

"There's nothing that can be done now." Will's voice is hard, like he wishes he didn't have to say what he did. "

"You could make her stop! Take away her weapons!" Sydney struggles in Will's grip.

"I took her gun. This is a hospital, and a lot of things can be used as weapons."

"Then lock her up!"

"I can't do that. If zombies break in, I can't worry about freeing everyone. Let it go." His face says the opposite, but he walks Sydney away toward the staff room to get Sara out of her sight.

As the crowd dissipates, Jim steps closer to Sara. "I think you made the right choice."

Once he walks away, Tyler approaches Sara. "Why did you have to kill her? You know she wasn't bit."

"I told you. We don't know how this works. Being touched could be enough to turn someone."

"Almost all of us have been touched, and we're not turning. It's like I don't even know you anymore with you acting like this." Tyler's heart aches.

"Maybe you didn't know me before any of this happened either."

Her words sting Tyler, but he pushes. "I'd like to think I did. You were strong. You cared for our daughter on your own when I was too much of a coward to help. You always offered help to anyone and your smile could make my whole day. I know times are dark right now, but I miss that smile."

"I cared for *my* daughter because I didn't have a choice. I didn't have the option to walk away and pretend it never happened." The hate sharpens her words.

"You told me you didn't want me in her life!!" It isn't the right time for this conversation, but Tyler can't stop himself. "You never gave me a chance to be her father. You didn't want people to know it was me you had a drunken one-night stand with. I've had to watch you raise her from afar for your benefit, not mine."

Tyler's words don't seem to have any effect on Sara. Her face stays neutral. "Why do you watch me so much?"

"Sara, I was in love with you. I had been for a long time. That night wasn't a mistake to me, it was the one thing I did right. The wrong part is when I let you walk away from it. I should have told you then. Maybe having someone to go through this disaster with would have helped you."

"Help me what? Help me die? Because caring for someone would just be a distraction. I can't be blinded by someone and save everyone else. That's why I can't care about Sydney's sympathy for a cat, or Lynn's hope for Mason. And I most certainly can't care about your pathetic profession of love."

Chapter Twelve

Day fifteen
Tiffany

Tiffany clutches the bottle of pills close to her body in hopes of keeping the rattling quiet. Will and Erin are preoccupied with Heather, so Tiffany takes the opportunity to creep into the empty office. The metal cabinet on the wall has the key in the lock. She looks over her shoulder one more time before dipping into the darkness.

Looking down at the bottle in her hand, Tiffany fights the back and forth war in her mind. *I don't need these.* She turns the key and eases the door open. Several bottles of controlled drugs line the shelves in alphabetical order. *But what if I do?* Her hand hovers in midair as she tries to push herself to set the bottle on the shelf.

In one deep breath, she summons all her willpower and forces herself to put the bottle down. Her exhale releases the tension building in her shoulders. *I won't need them. I'm over it.*

No more drugs. No more Brent. His hold over her should have left when she completed rehab. The haze of sex and drugs made her fall for him, but now she doesn't answer to a man like that. Not anymore.

Before closing and locking the door, she notices another bottle is missing. *Which one is it? A, B, C, D, E… Where's the euthanasia solution?* She dismisses the thought, assuming Will or Erin have it for Heather if things were to go south.

Her steps become easier the more she takes away from the office. Tiffany makes her way to the doctors hovering around isolation. Heather has been handcuffed to the kennels and monitored the past few days. An IV pump keeps her hydrated, and she eats when everyone else does.

Will gives her another handful of meds for the brain swelling, nausea, fever, and pain, anything to treat the symptoms since the disease itself isn't treatable yet. She should have turned yesterday or the day before. It took Carter a week to lose his humanity and according to Heather, that's how long it took for Colton to turn on her. She said she locked him up and hoped he would come to his senses, but his poundings eventually stopped. When she opened the bathroom door, she found Colton dead for no apparent reason.

The zombie captured for experiments in the runs died yesterday too. Even the area around the back door, where they constantly pound, is surrounded by dead bodies that weren't shot. From what everyone can tell, it seems they have a short amount of time. At least the humans do. The dog in the runs is still going strong and there are no random dog bodies outside. *But why?*

Heather looks up at the crowd around her. Her eyes are much brighter than the day she stumbled back here. "The meds have been helping. My thoughts are clearer than they have been, and the growling in my stomach has dulled. Do you think we're onto something?"

Will's shoulders relax. His words try to retain hopefulness. "It's too soon to tell, but maybe we are prolonging the change. It's a step in the right direction, at least."

"This isn't a cure. I think after the change, this would be useless." Erin's eyes are puffy and the dark bags under her eyes stand out more than Tiffany's seen before.

Heather nods and tries to reposition her handcuffed arm to be more comfortable. "When do you think I can be free again?"

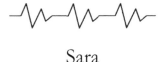

Sara

"Are you serious?" Sara stands at the back of the crowd hovering around Heather.

Will strides back to her. "Do not do anything out of line here, Sara." His voice is stern, but Sara doesn't even blink in his direction.

"She's infected! This time, you all even know it! You're going to just let her live and be a danger to all of us?" Sara watches her words bring tears to Heather's eyes, but it doesn't matter. The trick isn't going to work on her.

Will pulls Sara away from the group. "We are trying to make her better. A little hope from you would go a long way."

Sara stares Will dead in the eye. "I lost my hope with my daughter." She stalks away without looking back.

Sara bides her time, preparing everyone's meals with hotdogs, microwave mac and cheese, and corn. *We eat like royalty here.* Not that it was a bad meal, but Sara was growing tired of playing house and pretending all was fine. Something needed to change.

At dinner, everyone is unusually quiet. Maybe her outburst about Heather earlier made them all edgy. *Good.* Everyone needed to be alert, always. Getting comfortable here is going to get them all killed. The remaining eight, not counting Heather, can eat at the table in the staff room now, rather than on the floor in the treatment area.

Will stands in front of the group. "Erin and I have been talking, and we have a few things to share."

Erin nods and addresses the group. "When Lynn suggested the mosquitos we've been finding could potentially be causing the disease, my head snapped back to a recent article I read in one of the veterinary medical journals. It took me a while to find the article again, but here it is." She flashes the journal at the group then holds it in front of her to read. "According to the article, an experiment was being done to combine the Canine distemper and Rabies vaccines into one. The plan was then to put this vaccine into a carrier, the mosquitos, in order to disperse it among the wildlife in highly susceptible areas."

"If it's a vaccine, then why are the dogs and people acting crazed?" Tiffany asks.

"This tactic still had years of testing and legalities to go through. I think something went wrong, and the mosquitos were launched prematurely with lethal versions of the viruses. It would explain a lot of the symptoms we're seeing. The head tilts, muscle tremors, brain swelling, fever, etc."

"That would also explain how this seemed to explode all at once if hundreds of dogs were infected simultaneously," Sydney speculates between bites of food.

"Exactly," Will says. "We also need to discuss what we do next as a group. We realize we can't stay here forever. It doesn't look like help is coming, but that doesn't mean it's hopeless for us. Officer Chase talked about a radio in the police station. It should be able to reach twenty to twenty-five miles, and with the next town over only fifteen away, there's a good chance we could reach someone on the other end. Banning together with another group could mean more protection for all of us."

Some nod at the idea. Sara finds herself one of them. *At least someone else realizes we can't stay here.*

Will continues. "With the progress we are making on research and curing Heather, we may find others doing the same or that need our help with their own infected."

And that's where the similarities end. Sara frowns at the idea of toting around a potentially infected and hanging out with other infected. Maybe once they're out in the world, she can find a way to escape on her own. *A car would be nice.*

Will sits back down, and Sara excuses herself, claiming to take Heather her plate. Everyone stares at her as she goes to leave. She knows Tyler follows her, but she doesn't care. She just wants to talk for now.

In isolation, Heather stares at the wall. Sara approaches her carefully. Heather doesn't meet her stare.

"I brought you dinner," Sara mumbles. She hands over the flimsy paper plate.

Shock registers on Heather's face, but she takes the food. "Is it poisoned?"

Sara surprises herself with a laugh. "That would be way too much work. It's fine, I promise. I'd just use a gun if I came in here to kill you."

Heather flinches but begins to eat. "Why did you come in here?" She asks between mouthfuls.

"I'm on dinner duty today." Sara shrugs likes it's no big deal.

Heather hesitates but then continues to eat. Sara crouches down on the floor next to her and the two sit in silence for a few minutes. The dog in the runs barks, and a few answering barks come from near the back door. Soon, the familiar growls and scratches fill the quiet.

"They can sense each other," Heather says with a hollow voice.

"Huh?" Sara asks, having been lost in her own thoughts.

"The dogs and the zombies. They can all sense each other. Where they're at, what they need. It's not like reading their minds, exactly, but just knowing."

"How do you know that?"

"I was so close to turning. I could feel it. The presence of hundreds of other minds were in mine. It's like they were calling to me. Waiting for me." Heather shudders.

"And they're not there now?" Sara raises an eyebrow.

"No, not since the medicine has taken hold and I can think clearer. It's just me in here." She taps a finger against the side of her head.

"I guess that means something then." Sara clambers to her feet. "Enjoy your dinner." She leaves, shutting the door behind her.

Tyler

"Tyler, will you come with me to the police station?" Will's voice enters Tyler's mind as he stares at Sara from his familiar place in pharmacy. She stands outside of isolation with confusion written all over her face. She occasionally goes in to talk to Heather but always leaves within minutes. *What answers is she looking for?*

"Tyler?" Will puts a hand on Tyler's shoulder.

Tyler jumps and puts his hand on his gun. "What?"

Will takes his hand back. "I asked if you would go to the station with me. Are you okay?"

Tyler relaxes. "I'm fine. I was just thinking about Heather. Do you think we've really brought her back to normal? If we stop giving her the meds, will the infection take hold again?"

"I don't have all the answers. I wish I did. But for

now, it's working. And that's the best we've got to go on. I'm hoping we can get into contact with others, and maybe with more minds, we can sort this whole mess out."

Tyler nods. "So, we're leaving for the police station now?" He glances outside where the sun is setting behind the mountain.

"Yes. To conserve battery life for the radios, others most likely have set times they turn them on to talk. That could be sunset, sunrise, or noon. If we go now, we can hit sunset time and scan to see if we find anyone."

"How very *Walking Dead* of you to think that." Tyler chuckles.

The two men slip out the front door of the building since the dogs have been keeping an almost constant watch on the back door. Jake has to use the bathroom on puppy pads now since they can't risk taking him for walks outside anymore. They sneak down the hill toward the police station. Once inside the dark building, they both switch on their phone flashlights. Everyone had taken turns charging them on the two available chargers for the lights.

Down the hall to the room with the holding cell, the radio sits on a massive black desk. Everything looks to be there from when Officer Chase played with it the few times he came to check on Carter. He hadn't been able to reach anyone, but maybe he wasn't trying at the right times. *Hopefully.*

Will switches on the radio and flips through the fifteen channels, stopping to say "hello" on each. He waits a few seconds before switching to the next. Tyler leaves him to his channel surfing and takes a look around the rest of the building. He passes several offices and a staff room. It's been picked clean of anything edible from the various trips to check on Carter.

Will emerges form the back office and joins Tyler. "No luck this evening. We can try again in the morning."

Tyler nods and begins to leave the building, but Will puts his hand on his shoulder.

"Wait. There's a reason I asked you to come along."

Tyler stares at him quizzically. "A reason other than backup?"

"Yes. I could have asked anyone else to come along, but I specifically needed a man because I need your opinion."

Tyler shifts from foot to foot. "Opinion on what?"

"Jim." Will looks around as if someone could be listening, but no one else would be here other than the zombies. "Lynn and Sydney both feel uncomfortable around him. Lynn especially thinks he's got bad intentions with our group. I want to know if this is just the girls uncomfortable about a random man entering the group, or if the accusations have something to them."

Tyler bites at his lip. "Lynn had told me Jim said some weird things to her that made her uncomfortable. I brushed it off until Sydney said something similar. I also heard him tell Sara he agreed with her killing Josie." Tyler pauses before continuing, thinking of how to word the next part. "I also think he's stealing from us."

"Why do you think that?"

"I help Erin with the inventory. It helps to keep my mind busy, and there's been food coming up missing. She says she forgets to subtract our meals sometimes, but I don't. I keep a tab in my head, anything to not think about the zombies outside or about the girl I love turning into her own monster."

"Maybe we should have a talk with Jim soon. Do you have my back?"

"Of course. You're keeping us alive. I'll follow your lead on anything."

Will nods, and the two exit the building. They climb the hill back to the clinic without incident. Inside the lobby, Will stops Tyler again. "What you said back at the police station about me keeping everyone alive means a lot, but it's us as a whole that's done that. A lot have died too, and we can't forget that. Death does different things to different people. Sara is taking it especially hard. She's done things that we wish she hadn't, but her intentions are good at least. She may need someone like you to get through this, so don't give up on her yet. She's still in there somewhere."

"Thanks, Will." Tyler forces a smile but leaves to rejoin the others. *I don't think Sara is in there anymore.*

Sydney

Sydney listens as Jim rustles though his bag for what seems like the hundredth time. She doesn't have to see him to know what he's doing. She can lay on her makeshift bed in the treatment area and still hear him rummage in the staff room. Ever since her encounter with Carter in the laundry room, her senses have intensified. She's sure he infected her, so why isn't she turning?

She smells the oceanic tinge of the tuna can Jim just opened. Hears the swallows, as he indulges in a late-night snack. The soft snores from across the treatment area, where in isolation, Heather sleeps. She senses her. But she's wrong. Somehow

There's so many she senses outside. Some dogs, some human. They stalk around the building, waiting for a weak point. They call to her to join them, to let them in. But she's wrong too. They tell her that.

Jim rips open a pack of crackers, and Sydney finds herself unable to hold it in any longer. She throws off the thin blanket covering her body and slips through the darkness. Will stands guard in pharmacy, poised so he can keep an eye on the back door and the front door through the pharmacy door window.

When he sees Sydney approaching, he stands straighter. "What are you doing up? Is everything okay?"

Sydney shakes her head, quieting the growl wanting to claw up her throat. "No. Jim's up eating."

"Eating? How do you know?" Will's brows scrunch together.

"Because I can *hear* him." She hisses through her teeth. "He's eating our food, and he's been doing it every night since he's got here."

"Okay. I'll take care of it. Go back to bed."

Sydney hesitates, wondering if she should persist, but Will ushers her back to the other sleeping forms. He bends down at Tyler's bed and rouses him from sleep. They exchange a few words then walk off to the staff room together. When they turn on the light, it floods into the treatment area and pulls the others from their dreams.

"What's going on?" Lynn asks, her voice heavy with sleep.

"Will and Tyler are confronting Jim." Sydney's voice is flat. This has been coming.

Erin rises and looks as if she wants to assist but unsure how, so she just stands and waits.

Sydney's keen sense of hearing picks up on the conversation, although the voices start to rise. The others can probably hear the words as well.

"Jim, we have rules about rationing the food so we all stay fed as long as we can." Will's voice takes an authoritative tone.

"Are you denying a hungry man food?" Jim grunts. It sounds like his mouth is still full.

"We're all hungry. We eat to sustain ourselves, but you are overindulging. That puts us all at risk of running out of food. Our numbers are low, and making trips to look for food is costly. We need to be smart about this."

"I let you have a generator, the least you could do is give me food." Jim's voice raises in defense. Sydney imagines him backing into a corner with Will and Tyler staring him down.

"We're grateful for the generator, but without food for us all, what good will it do for our survival? If you can't see the necessity for rules in a situation like this, perhaps you would do better off on your own."

Sydney nods to herself. Jim has made her feel uneasy, and she knows others must feel the same.

"You're kicking me out to deal with those sons of

bitches out there on my own?"

"It seems that's the only choice we have unless you can follow the rules here."

A silence stretches on. Sydney can hear the heartbeats of the ones around her. They quicken as the moment continues.

Finally, Jim grumbles a response. "Well then I guess I'm leaving."

Sydney listens. He lifts something heavy, then he comes into view. He walks past the group of techs, Will and Tyler following close behind. Sydney launches to her feet, instinct taking hold. She stands between Jim and the back door. "Empty your bag first."

His eyes narrow at her small frame. "Get out of my way, little girl. Your leaders are kicking me out, so I'm leaving. End of it."

He tries to sidestep her, but she steps back in his path. "No."

Will and Tyler come up behind him and pull his backpack off his shoulders. Jim flips around and tries to snatch it back, but it's out of his reach. He fumes as he watches them open it. Will pulls out several cans of food, bottles of water, three pistols, and six bottles of antibiotics.

"Were you going to take all this stuff and skip out anyways?" Tyler asks, eyes wide at the man's stash.

"It's not like you didn't have enough to spare," Jim retorts, arms folded across his chest.

"That isn't the point." Will replaces one gun, half the cans and bottles, and one bottle of antibiotics. "We don't know how long we will be here. We offered you shelter and access to all these supplies, but you took advantage and were stealing from us. That's not okay.

I'm giving you supplies to survive until you find another group. Maybe by then, you'll learn to be smarter." He shoves the backpack back into Jim's arms.

The scruffy man stares at the doctor for a long moment, his cold eyes challenging him. Will stares back and the group of techs hold their breath for it to play out.

Finally, Jim backs away toward the door. "Fine. But you'll wish you had me when them things outside get in." He stomps his way out the door.

Will and Tyler replace the metal kennel behind him.

Lynn breathes a sigh of relief. The group all stare at each other for a long time. It had to be done, but the decision couldn't have been easy on Will.

What are we becoming?

Chapter Thirteen

Day sixteen
Tyler

Tyler and Will go back to the police station before dawn. They weave through the cars, taking the longer route down one driveway and up the other. The number of zombies and dogs looks like it's tripled over night.

"I think they know we're wanting to leave and they're planning to attack," Tyler says once they're safely inside the building.

"I hate the thought of them being able to think like that. Why can't they have the decency of being dumb zombies like in all the movies?" Will's attempt at a joke relaxes Tyler, if even just the smallest bit.

They sit in the same large office as the evening before and Will goes through the channels one at a time, pausing longer on each one, sometimes saying "hello" more than once.

Do you think there's anyone out there we can go to?" Tyler asks after five or six channels.

"Are you suggesting we're the last ones?" Will asks.

"No, there has to be more, but you know how in the zombie movies, the military sets up safe places… do you think they've done that?"

"But in the movies, aren't the military safe places usually overrun by the time the survivors get there?"

Tyler gives a small smile at the light banter. "True. But do you think there is somewhere safe we can go?"

"There has to be. This can't be the end. Humans fight too damn hard to go out with a whimper." Will switches to the next channel. "Hello? Is there anyone out there who can help? Hello?"

Silence.

Will reaches his hand up to switch to the next channel but a static voice comes through the radio. "Copy. Who is this? Over."

Tyler and Will stare at each other in shock. Will fumbles with the button on the radio. "Hello! This is Dr. Will Kennley at Second Chance Animal Hospital in Mercy County. Oh God, I can't believe we reached someone."

"How did you get on this channel? Over."

"We found a radio in the police station next door and have been trying channels during times we hoped someone would be listening. Where are you located?"

"This is Grace County police. We have a safe zone set up at the hospital. Are you the group with Officer Chase? Over."

Will's shoulders slump. "Yes, he was here with us, but we were overrun, and he was one that didn't make it."

Silence.

Tyler's heart pounds. They could shut off their radio. They could act like the group never contacted them and leave them on their own. If they tried to get to them, would they even let them in now? Do they blame them for letting one of their own die?

The policeman on the other end finally speaks again. "We can't send a rescue team. All our officers are devoted to keeping the ones here safe and finding supplies. If you can get to us, we will let you in. Over."

Both Tyler and Will breathe a sigh of relief, but uncertainty crosses Will's face. "I don't know how we will get to you. We're surrounded and every time we go out, we're swarmed."

"Find a car. Some of the ones left in locked garages haven't been tampered with. If you can get to one you can drive through them. Just let us know when you are on your way. How many are in your group? Over."

"There's nine of us. We're going to pack our supplies and leave right now."

"We won't let anyone in who looks or acts questionable, so make sure you know your group well. We have a lot of people here and we plan to keep them safe. At any cost. Over."

"Understood."

"We will see you soon. Over and out."

Will sets the radio down and runs a hand through his hair. Tyler knows he's thinking about Heather. She may not have turned, but is she still infected? He offers, "Maybe if you offer her condition as progress toward a cure, they'll let her live. They may have to lock her up somewhere for a while first…"

"What if they only see her as a threat, and our group as dishonest? Do I sacrifice the safety of the group for Heather's life?"

"You can't just leave her here to die, and you know that. If they don't let us in, we'll go somewhere else that will. Someone will have to listen somewhere."

Will nods. "You know, you make a great leader. I'm proud of how much you've grown up in these few weeks. I hope you're right."

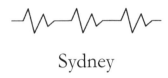

Sydney

Sydney can feel all eyes on her. She paces across the treatment area like a wolf trapped behind bars at a zoo. They're outside. Dozens of them. They're waiting. *We will have them all. Soon.* The voices send chills through Sydney. She should have turned by now. Will she ever?

The metal kennel against one of the doors leading to the lobby screeches against the floor as it's shoved open too fast. Erin and Tiffany advance toward the door with their pistols drawn. Sara hangs back further. Without her weapon, she still looks intimidating, but Sydney knows it's not the zombies. Not yet.

Will and Tyler skirt through the small opening and shove the kennel back into place, pushing their weight against it. "They're swarming!" Tyler's shout confirms Sydney's fears.

"How many?" Tiffany asks, checking her

magazine.

"Too many," Will says, locking the wheels on the kennel in place, making it harder to slide on the floor. "Everyone pack your backpacks with supplies. Food, water, medicine, ammo, anything important. We're leaving."

The techs begin scrambling to gather their things. Sydney goes for her own backpack but listens to Will and Erin's conversation. Erin follows close behind her husband as he makes his way toward isolation. "Where will we go? Did you reach someone on the radio?"

Will opens the door and reaches in his pocket for the key to Heather's handcuffs. "Yeah, I did. Grace County Hospital is safe. It's protected by a strong police force and there are other people there."

Grace County Hospital. That's where Spencer works. He could still be alive if the police made it a safe zone. Elation radiates through Sydney. But she's infected. Even though she hasn't turned yet, she could still put the entire place at risk. But she could see Spencer again.

To Sydney, Jake qualifies as important. While everyone is occupied with their own survival bags, Sydney swaddles Jake in a blanket and pushes him into her backpack. *Good thing he's a puppy.* He squirms but she clutches the bag against her in hopes to conceal the movement from the others. Her mission as a thirteen-year-old is finally complete.

Heather stands and rubs her wrists where the handcuffs had been. Will pulls her from the room. "Stay close to us. Don't get infected again, and when we get to the hospital, don't tell anyone about your condition until I can talk with them."

"Will they kill me if they know?" Heather asks, fear distinct in her voice.

"They've already said they would, but if I can get them to see this treatment is working, we could change their mind. Your survival is important. You're proof. You're hope."

Heather nods and goes to pack a bag of her own.

Erin again presses her husband for answers. "How will we get to the hospital? It's so far. We will be attacked before getting down to the main road."

"If we can find a car in a garage, we will be okay. The zombies most likely didn't get to those." Will starts to pack a bag of his own, filling it with guns and all the water he can cram inside. He addresses the group as a whole. "The more food and water we can bring, the better. We can offer it to the group we're—"

The three metal kennels blocking the doors come crashing to the floor with a loud bang. Zombies and dogs flood through the openings with one coming in behind Will. The mangled woman bites into the side of Will's neck before he has a chance to turn with his gun. Blood squirts and he screams in pain, knees buckling.

Erin draws her weapon and shoots the woman in the head before rushing to her husband. "Will! Oh God! Will, tell me what to do. What do you need? I can fix this."

Sydney pulls out her own gun and aims it at the wave of zombies pouring in. In quick succession, she takes down three coming through the door.

Tyler pulls a second gun from his backpack and hands it to Sara. "Just shout the zombies." She takes the gun and begins peppering the attackers.

Will coughs and his voice comes out in garbled

splutters as Sydney hears him talk to Erin. "Get everyone else out of here. Get them to the hospital."

"I'm not leaving you! We can cure you now, like we did Heather." Erin's voice raises with hysteria.

"Too late for me. You can't carry me. Get them safe. You can do this." The blood loss becomes too great, and Will falls into unconsciousness.

Erin shakes him then rubs her hands across his face. "Will! No! Wake up! I need you!" The tears stream down her face. A black dog runs up and sinks its teeth into Will's leg, ripping and pulling like it's a chew toy. Erin brings the butt of her gun down on the dog's head with a force that cracks its skull. The dog collapses.

Sydney approaches them and lays a hand on Erin's shoulder. The vet whips her head around, pointing her gun at the attacker.

Sydney doesn't flinch. "We have to go now. More are coming."

Erin looks back at her husband, pain filling her expression. Then, she gets up and aims her gun. "Will said to keep you all safe. I'm going to get you out." Determination hardens her face.

Tiffany

Tiffany fires several more shots, taking down two of the three dogs charging through the door. The third lunges at her. It knocks her off her feet. She puts her hand against its neck, holding its gnashing teeth away from her face and fires her gun. The ringing of the close shot hurts her ears, but she pushes the dog off and climbs to her feet.

Sydney brings Erin over. The doctor's face is red and splotchy. Tiffany saw the zombie take down Will, but now isn't the time to mourn. It's time to survive or die. No in between. "Erin, what do we do?"

Erin sets her face with a serious look. "We need to get outside. They will corner us in here. We need to get to a house with a garage and pray there's a car inside."

Tiffany nods and begins shooting at the zombies funneling in through the backdoor. "I'll make a path! Everyone else stay close!" She reloads her pistol with another magazine, repositions her backpack straps, and makes steady progress for the exit.

Outside, the clouds cover the sky and foreshadow the rain to come. Erin and Sydney aren't far behind. They stare at the door they just came through. All they can do is wait for the others to emerge and stop other zombies from going in.

Tyler runs out, carrying two gas containers. "Is everyone out? I splashed the place with gas. With so many of those things inside, we could blow them sky high and get a head start to get a car."

"Lynn, Sara, and Heather are still inside." Erin starts for the door.

"I'm out!" Lynn shouts as she stumbles through the doorway. "I think Heather was behind me."

Tyler puts his arm out in front of Erin. "You stay here, we need you. Make sure everyone's okay. I'll get Sara."

Tiffany puts a hand to her forehead and walks around one corner of the hospital, scouting for more zombies. When she's out of sight of the others, she pulls her backpack off her shoulders and unzips it. Tucked in between a change of clothes are several bottles from the controlled drugs cabinet. When Will told them to pack the essentials, she couldn't stop herself.

She pulls out the bottle labeled Diazepam and pours a few of the small yellow pills into her palm. She brings her hand to her mouth and throws her head back, forcing the pills down her throat. *Here's for keeping calm during the end of the world.*

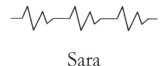

Sara

Sara approaches the staff room. Four dogs dive through the doorway, and Heather screams. The smaller doctor holds out a large kitchen knife, swiping it back and forth in the directions of the impending threats.

She spots Sara in the doorway, and relief floods across her face. "Thank God! I don't have a weapon. Can you help me?"

Sara raises her pistol, but instead of aiming it at one of the dogs, she points it at Heather.

"What are you doing?" Heather's eyes grow wide.

"You're a threat to our group. If we try to enter the hospital with you, they will turn us away. We'll be left to the mercy of these things."

"But I'm getting better. We're finding a cure! Will said I'm the important proof they need that we're on to something." One of the dogs snaps at Heather's leg but misses.

"There's plenty more zombies out there. Ones we don't have to risk being cooped up in a car with." Sara's expression doesn't waver.

"I thought you accepted I was getting better when we last talked." Heather's voice is hysteric as she tries to back further away from the dogs.

"You told me the dogs were in your head. You and I both know neither canine distemper nor rabies works like that. We're not curing you. We're just prolonging the inevitable. Whatever this disease is, it's going to change you."

"Why are you just after me? What about Sydney?'

"What *about* Sydney?" Sara narrows her eyes.

"When I first came here and was on the verge of turning, I could sense her. I could sense the dogs and the zombies, but I could sense her, in this hospital. That would have to mean she's infected too."

"Sydney wasn't bit." Sara's voice loses some confidence, but she doesn't lower her gun. Instead she fires, hitting Heather in the thigh.

Heather drops her knife and falls to her knees, clutching the wound. The dogs pounce at her. She tries to shove them away, but one by one they land bites on her arms, hands, and stomach.

Sara watches only a moment longer before turning away. Tyler stands a few feet away glaring at her. "I came to help get you two out. We're sending this pace up in flames." His voice is flat.

"I'm coming. Heather didn't make it." Sara only half-wonders if he saw the whole thing. *It doesn't matter.*

Tyler only nods. Sara follows behind him to the outside where the rest of her group waits. Tyler sets a few paper balls on fire with a lighter and tosses them into the building. The flames spread as they feed on the gasoline soaking every surface.

The group quickly retreats down the driveway, and as the flames reach the propane tank outside, the building behind them erupts with a deafening bang.

Chapter Fourteen

Day sixteen
Tyler

The rain pummels Tyler's head, soaking through his clothes. His wet shaggy hair sticks to his forehead. The fire behind them still blazes even through the rain, sending pillars of dark smoke into the cloud covered sky.

When the group reaches the highway, Erin looks back and forth in indecision. "I don't know which way we should go. Will should be here instead of me. He was better at snap decisions."

Tyler reaches her side. "Let's head to Chris's house. I have his keys, and I think he has a truck in the garage." Tyler produces Chris's keychain from on the counter in pharmacy. When packing to leave, he decided the trinkets fell under the category of important.

"You're a genius, Tyler." Erin gives his arm a squeeze and they head down the road toward Grace County.

Chris didn't live too far, thankfully, and they reach his house without incident thanks to the distraction of the explosion. Tyler unlocks the front door and they creep through the house. Erin instructs everyone to grab anything useful they find while she follows Tyler to the garage.

A dark blue, newer model Chevy with a bed cap takes up most of the space. Erin opens the drivers' side door and Tyler hands her the keys. "I know losing Will is hard for you. I can't imagine. I liked him for his leadership and confidence. But he isn't here now. That means you have to step up and take his place. Everyone in this group looks up to you."

Erin lowers her gaze but then nods her head. "You're right. Thank you, Tyler."

"I've got your back." He gives her a small smile.

The rest of the group files into the garage with their backpacks overly stuffed. The seating arrangement will be cramped but Tyler stops the progression. "Wait. We need to talk."

Erin looks at Tyler with her head cocked to one side. The same look of confusion crosses the others' faces. Everyone's but Sara's.

Tyler takes a deep breath. Will wanted him to be a good leader. He knows he has to protect the group no matter the cost. Even if the cost breaks his heart. "I don't think Sara should come with us."

"What?" The outrage is plain on Sara's face.

Erin steps forward, closing in our small circle. "We

can't just leave her here."

"I know Sara has good intentions about keeping this group safe. She's a fighter. But she's too impulsive. She doesn't stop to think anymore."

"And to think you were just professing your love for me only last week." The venom coating Sara's words makes Tyler flinch.

Tyler ignores her and forces the next words out, knowing they need said. "She shot Heather back at the clinic and left her to die."

Erin's eyes widen. "Sara?"

"She was infected!"

"But we were curing her!" Lynn steps away from her place beside Sara.

"So, what then? Are you all just going to send me out on my own like you did Jim?" Sara folds her arms across her chest.

Erin thinks about the decision that needs to be made. Tyler can't read her expression and wonders what she's going to do. *What would Will do?*

"Everyone get in the truck." Erin opens the drivers' door again and slides into the seat.

"You're letting her come with us?" Lynn asks in horror.

"I won't force one of our own out. I can't. She's done a lot of bad things, but we've lost too many people already. Will told me to keep everyone safe, and that's what I will do, or I will die trying. When we get to the hospital, I'm sure there will be stricter rules we may have to follow. I can't protect Sara there, but I can protect her here. Now get in the truck and let's go." She shuts the door.

Lynn looks like she wants to argue further, but she

just lets her shoulders slump and moves toward the truck.

Tyler opens the back-glass window and tosses his backpack, and some of the others, into the bed of the truck. He pushes the button for the automatic garage door and hops into the front passenger seat with Erin. When everyone else is in, she starts the truck with Chris's keys and pulls out onto the main road.

The rain beating down, and the windshield wipers, are the only noise for the ride.

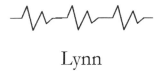

Lynn

Lynn stretches her legs. She opted to sit, unrestrained, in the bed of the truck. The back window of the cab is open, so she isn't completely secluded from the others, but she's happy to not be cramped in between them.

What if Daniel went to the hospital too? The same question replays over and over in her head as she lets the fear rise inside her chest. If the hospital is the safest place in the area, and if Daniel is still alive, that's where he will be.

Lynn opens her backpack and looks through her supplies, taking a mental inventory. Aside from bringing some food and water like the others, she also packed extra medicine, bandages, toiletries, and clothes. She refused to think about living under Daniel's rule again. If that meant running away on her own, she would do just that. But also tucked at the bottom is a bottle of euthanasia solution and a syringe.

She allows herself to think of the alternative.

Daniel is probably dead. They could arrive at the hospital and be greeted warmly by a group of survivors bent on creating a community that protects and cares for each other. She could find friends. Maybe family, even. Maybe she could fall in love like she thought she was with Mason. The possibilities of a new life make her heart flutter and brings a smile to her face.

But then it disappears.

Daniel would fight to survive. Mason is dead. Sara killed him. And she's going to be at the hospital. Lynn would have to continue to see her and think of Mason. All. The. Time.

When have things worked in her favor? When hasn't this apocalypse taken the opportunity to screw her? She clutches her backpack tighter to her chest then makes her decision. She pulls out the glass bottle holding her vibrant pink liquid answer. Before they arrive at the hospital, she'll already be gone. Free of this maddening reality.

Sydney

Grace County Hospital is only a half hour away, but the trip feels much longer. Sydney sits in the backseat of Chris's truck with Tiffany and Sara. Luckily, she scored a window seat so she could watch the dreary green landscape blur by the window. Tiffany was too out of it to argue about being crammed in the middle seat. *Is she just that tired?*

Sara sits at the other window seat, and Sydney tries hard to ignore the sidelong glares she keeps shooting her. *What's her deal? What did I do?*

Sydney averts her attention back to the window. She sees a few zombies and dogs dotted along the way. They seem to be walking, but she knows they have a purpose. All of them. With her backpack unzipped just a crack, her hand absentmindedly strokes Jake's fur. So far, he's stayed quiet and still. *I'm infected and I'm smuggling in a dog. No one would ever trust me if they knew.*

The truck accelerates as Erin pushes the gas pedal down. She seems anxious to reach the hospital. She probably thinks the sooner she gets there, the sooner she doesn't have to look after the whole group alone anymore. Losing Will hit her hard. They worked so well together, able to bounce ideas off each other until they solved the problem. But he was the leader. She's a half of a whole now.

The tall grey hospital stands a little outside of town. The intimidating fence surrounding the building is new. So are all the men with guns walking its perimeter.

As Erin nears, one officer approaches the truck with his hand held up in a stop position. Erin obeys and rolls down her window.

The man comes up beside the truck and peers in at the group. "You the ones from Mercy? The animal hospital?"

"Yes. There's six of us," Erin says, clearly trying to hide the pain behind those words.

There were fifteen employees at Second Chance Animal Hospital the day the outbreak happened. Now there's six. That means nine died. And that's not counting Officer Chase, or the clients who happened to be in the building at the time, or the animals caught in the middle of it all, like Josie. Thinking of the numbers makes Sydney feel sick. She cracks her window, letting the cold rainy air smack her in the face.

Of the six who survived, none of them were who they were. While trapped the past two and a half weeks, they've all changed. They've become fierce, smarter, and lethal. But they've also become cold. How many has Sydney killed?

The officer radios their arrival to someone in command and he waves them through, instructing us to park near the main entrance and talk to the man behind the desk.

Erin nods and does as he says. The group exits the truck and grabs their bags. Everyone except Lynn. Erin assumed she fell asleep, so she lets her be for now. They walk together as the last survivors to the automatic doors of the hospital. The reception opens and a large desk sits at the right. A man in military uniform stands to greet them, his hand outstretched to Erin. *We're going to be okay here.*

No sooner the thought crosses Sydney's mind does a sharp pain fill her head. She drops to her knees and clutches her head. She tries to swallow the scream wanting to escape her lips. Whimpers slip through, and Erin and Tyler rush to her side. They put their hands on her, asking her what's wrong and try to help her stand.

The military man raises his voice, demanding to know if Sydney had been infected. Erin leaves her side to assure him she hadn't but quickly brings her attention back to her tech.

Sydney tries to move her lips to make the words come out. Blurs of each of her friends come in and out of focus.

"What did you say?" Erin asks, bending her ear close to Sydney's lips.

Sydney swallows and tries again, knowing she has to get the message out. The message from the hundreds of voices screaming in her mind. Her voice cracks but she forms the words in strangled sobs. "They're coming." Her heart thumps, increasing the pressure in her chest. Her ears drum with the sound of her blood pulsating through her veins. "They're coming to change us. All of us."

Acknowledgments

Firstly, I want to thank you, the reader, for choosing my book to read. Your support in my writing dreams means the world. If you could do me one more favor and leave a review, I would be most grateful!

I also want to thank my tech support fiancé, Anthony. Without him, I wouldn't have a website, blog, formatted book, social media promo pictures and videos, the list goes on. I'd be lost. So, thank you, and I love you.

I want to thank my beta readers for their early insight.

Thank you to my editors Meg Trast at Overhaul My Novel and C. D. Tavenor at Two Doctors Media.

Thank you to my cover designer, Michele Sagan for an amazing job on this beautiful over and for my social media banners.

Thank you to the Writing Community of Twitter. You all make me feel welcomed and supported every day.

Lastly, thank you to all of you who believed in this book even when I didn't. Your push and encouragement is what completed this project.

I couldn't have made it this far without all of you. So, thank you.

About the Author

Ashley Nicole lives in a small town in West Virginia with her fiancé and spoiled kitten, River. By day, she works at her local vet clinic and by night she pours her imagination out onto a page. She has dreamed of becoming a published author for so long and has finally made it a reality. She has plans for dozens of other stories ranging from fantasy to dystopian to thriller and she hopes you'll come along for the ride!

You can keep updated on new book and writing tips by visiting www.ashleynicolewrites.com. Connect with her on her social medias Twitter, Facebook, Instagram, and Pinterest.

As a writer, Ashley's goal is to share everything she learns on her author journey. She posts regular writing tip articles on her Medium profile.